"You look beautiful. Every guy in the place is going to be praying you win him. Except me, of course."

"Did you just compliment and insult me in the same sentence?"

"Not at all. I excluded myself from the prayerful because you said you couldn't afford me. Did you get all dolled up just to watch the bidding on me? I'm touched. Especially when *you* could have had a date for free."

"Actually, I was considering bidding.... A dollar seemed a good estimation of your value. Then again...who knows? I might win. Decided it wasn't worth the risk."

Kate Denton is a pseudonym for the Texas writing team of Carolyn Hake and Jeanie Lambright. Friends as well as co-authors, they concur for the most part on politics and good Mexican restaurants, but disagree about men—tall versus short—and what constitutes good weather: sun versus showers. One thing they do agree on, though, is the belief that romance is not just for the young!

The Bachelor Bid
Kate Denton

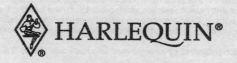

HARLEQUIN®

TORONTO • NEW YORK • LONDON
AMSTERDAM • PARIS • SYDNEY • HAMBURG
STOCKHOLM • ATHENS • TOKYO • MILAN • MADRID
PRAGUE • WARSAW • BUDAPEST • AUCKLAND

ISBN 0-373-17403-9

THE BACHELOR BID

First North American Publication 1998.

CHAPTER ONE

CARA BREEDON had reached the door of her boss's office, about to make her exit, when Brooke Abbott's voice halted her in her tracks. "By the way...any progress with Wyatt McCauley?"

Give me strength—not McCauley again! To Cara, the name was starting to grate like nails on a chalkboard. Just to get through one day—even one morning—without hearing that name, that question. No such luck. "Not much headway yet," Cara reluctantly answered.

"Then you've got to get cracking, Cara. I *want* Wyatt McCauley."

Tell me something I don't know. Ever since Brooke's designation as chair of her sorority's celebrity bachelor auction, she'd fixated on the idea of computer magnate McCauley as the star attraction. Having delegated to Cara, her secretary, the task of making her fixation a reality, Brooke had reserved for herself the chore of spewing out reminders and demanding updates.

Brooke would have gone after McCauley herself if it hadn't been for the fact her firm, Brooke Abbott Advertising, had just signed its biggest client to date.

The curse of good fortune meant that all of Brooke's energies had to be directed toward the new client.

Still, she somehow managed to eke out a few minutes each day to yank Cara's chain about McCauley. For the past two weeks every other sentence from Brooke had been "Wyatt-this, Wyatt-that." With each new mention of him, Cara's suspicions became that much firmer that when Brooke said she wanted the man, she wasn't talking only about the auction. She wanted Wyatt McCauley, period. And she wanted him bad. Were it within Cara's power, she'd deliver him—gift-wrapped or hog-tied if necessary—just to get Brooke off her case.

Landing McCauley wasn't the first difficult project Cara had been handed, but it *was* proving to be the most exasperating. As she drove home from the office Cara tried to keep in mind that Brooke was a generous employer, paying top dollar to her staff. In return she expected lots of late evenings and Saturdays, plus a myriad of personal tasks that had nothing to do with company business. On the whole, Cara didn't mind. It wasn't unusual for a company owner to throw in such additional duties. If it meant pleasing the boss, she could tolerate picking up her dry cleaning and doing the grunt work for a favorite Abbott charity. All in all, Cara had few complaints. Few complaints, that is, until the day Brooke first uttered the words "auction" and "McCauley" in the same sentence. Now the job was turning into a gigantic headache.

The problem was Wyatt McCauley wasn't cooperating. For the past ten days, Cara had called his office only to find him unavailable each time. Just yesterday she tried again, surprised when she'd been put straight through to the man himself.

"Cara Breedon, Mr. McCauley. Thank you for taking my call," she had begun.

"No problem," McCauley had answered cordially. "It's been such a hectic day, I welcome an excuse to escape the pile of work on my desk—now you've given me one."

They'd chatted amiably for a minute or so before he pressed the point. "And what may I do for you, Ms. Breedon?"

There had been no innuendo in his soft Texas accent, but still Cara could just imagine what he could do. The voice alone was enough to help Cara understand Brooke's fanatical interest.

"I'm recruiting participants on behalf of Brooke Abbott, chair of the Rosemund bachelor auction. You're probably aware that the auction benefits—"

A loud sigh had stopped her spiel. "Ms. Breedon, too bad you've wasted your time and mine. As I've told your auction gang repeatedly, I don't do that sort of thing. Good day." The line had clicked off.

Cara remembered staring at the receiver by then humming with a dial tone. She had been tempted to dial McCauley back and tell him just what she thought of his manners. He'd been so nice at first until she...until she'd taken advantage of his accessibility with a sales pitch, one he'd apparently heard once too often. Grudgingly Cara had admitted that yes, he did have the right to cut her off.

But, darn it, she thought now, she had to have this man and she'd keep after him until he said yes. Somehow she needed to make him understand that the auction wasn't "that sort of thing" but an important fund-raiser for a worthy cause.

It was either keep after McCauley or report failure to Brooke. And at the moment, she'd do anything to avoid such a scenario. Caught between the new big-fish client and the fast-approaching auction, Brooke was so uptight she might commit hara-kiri—or ask Cara to.

The next morning Cara called McCauley's office again. The assistant said the CEO was tied up and couldn't speak with her. Cara left a message asking that he ring her back. Three days passed with no return call.

Casting about for a different approach, Cara decided to adopt a marketing strategy, beginning with the gift of a bright-red, limited-edition sports cap publicizing the auction. Along with the cap went a letter explaining the cause it benefited—the Rosemund Learning Center for disadvantaged children.

Neither the cap nor the letter elicited a response, so Cara followed up with a tie—special delivery from the Neiman-Marcus flagship store in Dallas. The enclosed card said she hoped to "tie up his support for the auction." Still no reaction.

After the tie, which she now envisioned twisted tightly around his neck, Cara tried sending Wyatt lunch from her favorite Mexican restaurant, having heard through the grapevine that he was an aficionado of Austin's heralded "Tex-Mex" cuisine.

Since targeting his head and neck had proved unsuccessful, Cara was aiming lower, following the adage that the way to a man's heart was through his stomach. The lunch, with an accompanying written plea nestled among the dessert of pecan pralines, proved a washout as well. No contact. No "Thank you very much, the food was delicious." No anything. Cara's murderous thoughts were multiplying.

With Brooke badgering her relentlessly, Cara opted for another telephone call. She was informed "a check is in the mail." Cara mouthed a silent expletive. McCauley could send over his entire fortune in an armored truck and it wouldn't get Brooke off her back. He was missing the point here.

The check arrived—a substantial contribution— along with a terse, typed note that he simply wasn't interested in taking part. Maybe the poor guy thought that if he put it in writing, the message would finally get through.

Cara suffered another twinge of conscience. She'd been so zealous carrying out Brooke's mandate that she'd overlooked the fact she was practically harassing this man. Wyatt McCauley probably thought her and everyone associated with the auction a collection of crazies who couldn't grasp the simple meaning of "no." In fact, she'd begun questioning her own sanity for continuing this ridiculous campaign rather than pleading with Brooke to give up or assign the job to someone else. But no telling how a stressed-out Brooke would react to such a request.

Having tried everything she could think of short of plotting a kidnapping, Cara decided to seek out the lion in his lair. If she showed up in person she could appeal to his sensitive side—assuming that he had one—and perhaps persuade him to reconsider.

Wyatt's lair was an office in downtown Austin, not far from the state capitol. As she drove by in her aging Volkswagen Jetta, Cara noticed the trees now in full bloom, the capitol grounds teeming with camera-toting tourists and nearby office workers out for a breath of fresh spring air.

She managed to find a parking space, deposited several coins in the meter, and started toward Wyatt's building. On the way she spotted a florist on the corner. Flowers? What the heck, this was a go-for-broke mission. She entered the store.

"A dozen of the yellow roses, please...no, make that two dozen." Brooke had told her to do whatever was necessary. Perhaps the flowers would help sway the man...or at least gain her entrance to his inner sanctum.

"Cara Breedon to see Mr. McCauley."

"I'm afraid that's impossible, Ms. Breedon." The woman, Frances Peters, Executive Assistant—according to the nameplate on the desk—was courteous and efficient, but offering no encouragement. Still, Cara could have sworn there was a hint of amusement in her expression as she eyed the cellophane-wrapped roses. "I believe Mr. McCauley has made—"

"Frances—oh, excuse me, I didn't know you had someone with you." He turned to Cara. "May I cut in a minute, miss?" Without waiting for assent, he turned back to the assistant. "I need the time difference between here and Melbourne."

"I'll look it up." Frances Peters swiveled toward a bookcase and removed an almanac.

"Sorry," he said, focusing his attention on Cara as Frances studied the almanac.

This was Wyatt McCauley. No wonder Brooke was in such a dither over the man. Cara had seen pictures of him in the business and society pages, but while the grainy photos had shown a handsome man, they'd failed to capture the essence. The nondescript eyes shown in the pictures were actually a heat-seeking brown, his dark hair as glossy as a raven's wing, and the wide apologetic smile now directed her way seemed capable of illuminating a room, maybe a football field. McCauley might have made his mark in computers, but this was no stereotypical computer nerd.

He was coatless, starched white shirt with sleeves rolled to the elbow, navy pin-striped trousers and... well—what do you know?—*her* tie. Score one for her side. She knew she was staring—gawking, actually— but then, he was giving her the once-over, too.

No doubt less impressed than she. Wyatt McCauley was a ten, a ten plus, and she...six might be stretching it somewhat. Certainly Cara couldn't compete in the McCauley league, not with the glamorous women he squired around.

Likely, Wyatt McCauley's steady perusal of her was motivated by curiosity at discovering a woman in his waiting room clutching twenty-four roses to her bosom, or by the fact he simply had nothing better to do at the moment. It would be presumptuous of her to read any special interest into it.

"Sixteen hours difference, Mr. McCauley," said Frances.

"Thanks. Again, sorry for the interruption," he said to Cara.

Her reveries now under control, Cara snapped to attention. She couldn't believe she'd frittered away precious minutes in slack-jawed adulation instead of taking advantage of the perfect opportunity to pitch the auction. Fortunately it wasn't too late to rectify her lapse.

She shoved the flowers toward him. "Actually, you weren't interrupting. These are for you. I'm Cara Breedon."

Obviously taken by surprise at having been waylaid by the very person who'd hounded him for weeks, Wyatt's hands closed reflexively around the bouquet and he stared at it for a second.

"I'm sorry, Mr. McCauley," Frances said. "I told her you weren't available—"

"It's okay." Wyatt transferred the flowers to

Frances. "Put these in some water. I suppose I can spare a few minutes," he said resignedly. "Since Ms. Breedon's gone to so much trouble." He motioned Cara to join him in his office.

As she entered, she noticed the breathtaking view of Town Lake from his wall of windows, then the beautiful office itself. Functional—computer on the right side of his desk, multi-button phone on the left, open briefcase overflowing with documents resting on the credenza behind. And decorative—southwestern artwork displayed on two walls, a lifelike wood sculpture of cowboy boots standing in a corner, and a gold-leaf framed photo of two smiling Irish setters next to the briefcase.

Closing the door, he commented, "Perhaps I should recruit you for my sales force. I doubt I've met anyone, male or female, with as much tenacity."

"Somehow I suspect that wasn't meant as a compliment. Please be assured I'm not trying to be annoying, Mr. McCauley," Cara said in what she hoped was a soothing tone.

His cagey look said she didn't have to *try* to be annoying, still he offered her a chair. Cara sat down and Wyatt propped a hip on the corner of his desk, one long leg straightened in front of him to bear his weight. The fact that he didn't take a seat sent an unspoken reminder: Don't squander another second.

"It's just that Brooke Abbott and I strongly believe in the Rosemund Learning Center and what it's doing with kids," Cara began. "Because the Center receives no government funds, it's totally dependent on the goodwill of people like yourself. The bachelor auction is the major fund-raiser.''

Wyatt reached across the desk, and retrieved a checkbook. ''No argument here. I've read a lot about the organization and I agree it's making a difference. I'll be happy to—''

''You've already sent a check.''

''Obviously more is needed. Or you wouldn't be here.'' He pulled a pen from a gold pen and pencil set and started scribbling, signing his name with a flourish.

''I'm not here for another check,'' Cara protested. ''It's the auction that's on my agenda.''

He slapped his thigh in frustration. ''What part of my refusal didn't you understand, Ms. Breedon? Are you dense or just pathetically stubborn? Any idiot should have figured out by now that hell will freeze over before I go parading around in front of an audience of man-hungry women admiring my tush.''

''Admiring,'' he'd said, as if it were a given. He was right, of course—everyone would be admiring. Undoubtedly he was used to approval, not just of his backside, but from any imaginable angle.

For a few moments there in his anteroom, she'd been pretty appreciative herself. After his outburst, however, all idolizing had drained away, victim to his insolent refusal. She felt no more remorse for bothering him either. At that moment all she felt was aggravation at this galling display of ego.

"I can see it now," he quipped. "A group of us guys prancing around like performers in a male strip joint. My turn comes. I strut my stuff until a voice cries out, 'Five bucks for the guy in the purple briefs.'"

"Purple briefs—you?" Cara taunted, raising one eyebrow. For a second, her brain reeled off a picture of Wyatt in purple underwear—dollar bills stuffed in the waistband as he danced before a bunch of screaming, applauding women.

Her thoughts were cut off by Wyatt's terse, "No comment. Neither you, your boss, nor anyone else connected with that auction will find out, because I intend to hold on to every atom of my dignity."

"You disappoint me," Cara said.

"Why? Because I'm not willing to be part of your beefcake parade?"

"No, because you haven't done your homework. It's not a strip show. The participants wear tuxes, not skimpy garb. And you needn't worry about your monetary value being bounced back and forth for all to hear. It's a silent auction."

"I'm not a bit worried, and it doesn't matter what kind of show you're promoting, because I don't intend to be there." He rubbed the back of his neck wearily. "Listen, lady, I've been hit on about this for the last three years and my answer has always been the same. Why don't you people give it up?"

Cara sidestepped the question with a question of her own. "Don't you want to be known as the most eligible bachelor in Austin?'' She was losing steam here, but wouldn't give up without a fight.

''A few people have already tried to label me with that tag. All it means is that I'm over twenty-one, single, and have money in the bank. Big deal.''

''Only a few?'' Cara sniped, then caught herself. What was she doing? It wouldn't do her cause any good to irritate this man further. Not when he already saw her as a major nuisance. Her only hope was to get back on course—mature, businesslike. Even though anxiety had her ready to climb the walls.

Surprisingly he smiled, as if he found her retort amusing. But his resolution was firm. ''Like I said, I'm happy to make a contribution—of money, not my body.'' He tore off the check he'd written and dangled it toward Cara.

''I don't want another check, darn it. I want you!''

Wyatt lay the check down. He gave her a long appraising stare potent enough to raise the hairs on Cara's neck. ''That sounds promising,'' he drawled.

''You know I didn't mean it that way, that I...I was referring to the auction.'' Cara seldom blushed, but she felt her face flushing to a scarlet hue. She fantasized about diving under McCauley's big oak desk, or better still, sprinting out of here at full throttle.

The saving buzz of the intercom provided her a moment's respite from flushes and fantasies. ''Sure, I'll take it,'' Wyatt said. ''Just ask him to hold on a second.'' He pressed off the intercom button and turned his attention to Cara. "This has been... pleasant, Ms. Breedon, but I've got an important call coming through." He stood up and pushed the check toward her. "By the way, thanks for the tie." He fingered it casually. "Also the food and the flowers." He paused. "And if you change your mind about wanting me...for anything other than the auction..."

Cara snatched the check. At least she'd come away from this encounter with something for the kids. But she couldn't allow Wyatt's remark to go unanswered. "Just to set the record straight, Mr. McCauley, *I'm* not the one who wants you. It's my boss, Brooke Abbott. She's convinced the auction is doomed without you. I may disagree..." Cara's expression suggested that in her mind his involvement was about as important to the children's future welfare as chicken pox. "But Ms. Abbott's chairing the auction this year and she sees you as the pièce de résistance, a cinch to generate sky-high bids."

"Then relay this to your boss," Wyatt said, "and you can quote me. It doesn't matter if the bids are projected to reach a million dollars—I'm not going to do this." He stood up. "And that's my final word on the subject."

When he took her arm and ushered her toward his door, tingles ran through Cara's body. The closeness, the feel of his warm fingers against her skin, made her long for something she couldn't name. As the door closed behind her, she felt unaccountably empty, disillusioned—defeated. "Hemlock cocktail, any-one?" she muttered.

"Pardon?" Frances asked, observing Cara carefully.

"Nothing...sorry." Cara quickly exited through the frosted-glass doors and headed toward the elevator, wishing she could drive directly home and jump into bed with the covers over her head, rather than go back to the office and Brooke's displeasure.

She'd just pushed the down button when Frances Peters walked up behind her. "Don't give up hope," the woman whispered. "Maybe he'll have second thoughts." Without another word, Frances swept down the hall and disappeared into the ladies' room.

Fat chance, Cara answered silently. *I know a lost cause when I see one.*

Twilight had long gone before the day's business dealings came to a close. Lifting his eyes from the computer screen, Wyatt saw it was dark outside, his scenic view replaced by the spangled glow of city lights. He rose from his leather desk chair, stretched, rolled down his shirtsleeves and grabbed his jacket. Time to go home. Briefcase in hand, he opened his office door.

Frances was still at her computer. Wyatt glanced at his watch disapprovingly. "Gad, woman, it's eight o'clock. Why in blazes are you still here?"

"Most bosses complain that their assistants leave too early. Mine grouses because I work too late."

"Well, you're stopping right now. I don't want you in the building all alone," Wyatt told her. "Get your purse and I'll walk you to your car."

Frances smiled agreeably, closed the document file, and shut down the computer. As she circled her desk, she bent to smell one of the yellow roses Cara Breedon had brought earlier. They were now arranged in a Waterford vase. "Pretty, aren't they? Sure you don't want to take them home, enjoy them over the weekend?"

"You take them, if you like. For all I care they can go in the trash."

"Such a shame." Frances picked up the vase and cradled it in her left arm. "It's not like you to take out your bad moods on some lovely—"

"Don't push it, Frances," Wyatt growled as they started toward the elevator.

"All I was going to say was 'flowers.'" She smiled again, obviously unruffled by his admonition and the glare he shot her way.

Frances had worked for Wyatt for almost a decade and a half, beginning when McCauley Industries was just getting off the ground, its owner an undergrad hawking computer software to fellow classmates at the University of Texas.

In the ensuing years, the operation had expanded beyond the college crowd and into a national conglomerate. During those same years, Frances had become more than an assistant to Wyatt. To him she was a confidante, a friend, a mother figure. Which meant that she felt perfectly free to meddle in his personal life and to offer unsolicited advice.

Fortunately for Wyatt, the elevator came quickly and was occupied by another late worker, so any further discussion of Cara Breedon's visit was dropped.

He might have been rescued from Frances's meddling, but now, as Wyatt drove toward his home in the Tarrytown area of Austin, he couldn't keep his thoughts from returning to Cara.

The fact was, he'd begun to delight in her campaign of persuasion, to wonder what she'd come up with next. Today's face-to-face encounter had been unexpected, but he'd savored the good-natured sparring. She was sweet, but not too sweet—just the right amount of tang there.

Most of the women he dated were more beautiful, more sophisticated, yet there was something appealing in her natural manner and her girl-next-door prettiness. Her soft honey-colored hair fairly begged for a man's touch and those matching tawny eyes almost had Wyatt assenting to the auction or anything else she might suggest. Cara Breedon was the kind of woman who pulled at a man's heartstrings. Precisely the kind of woman to stay away from.

CHAPTER TWO

"HI, SIS," two voices sang in unison as Cara dragged through her front door that evening. She dropped onto the couch, slipping out of her high heels and propping her aching feet on the coffee table. "Hi," she said unenthusiastically. "Hello, Flake," she said in the same voice to the white cat who'd sprung into her lap.

"What's wrong?" Mark asked. He undraped himself from his chair and deposited an apple core into the wastebasket.

"Yes, you look like you've lost your best friend," Meg added. "What's the problem?"

Cara gave her brother and sister a wan smile. Ever since Brooke had gotten on the Wyatt kick, Cara had been complaining to her siblings about her doomed crusade. "What else? Wyatt McCauley, the bane of my existence. I've tried every maneuver I can think of to get him to agree to that dratted auction. I'm flat out of ideas. You two got any brilliant suggestions?"

"Maybe you should just ask him to do it as a personal favor to you..." Meg said, batting her eyes exaggeratingly.

"Maybe I should make *you* ask him." Cara shook her head at Meg's antics.

"No way. But what's wrong with your using a more personal touch?"

"Meg, the man only knows me well enough not to like me very much. He thinks I'm...well, I'm not sure what he thinks, only it's not good. But Flake likes me, don't you, sweetums?" The cat butted its head against Cara's hand to demand she scratch his ears.

"If the guy knew as much about babes as he does computers, he'd think you were a complete wow," Mark defended.

"Thanks, honey, but I'm not the wow type, especially to men like McCauley—who, by the way, is no slouch in the looks department. Gorgeous women by the score are just begging to have their numbers entered in his personal Rolodex. There's no space for someone who's merely average, like me."

"Quit underrating yourself, Cara. You've got a lot going for you. Smart...pretty."

"And a brother who's prejudiced."

"No, for once in his life, Marko's on target," Meg joined in. "You *are* date bait. You just need to get out more, to mingle. All you do is work and take care of us. It's not fair to you."

"I like taking care of you." Cara had been doing so for the past seven years, ever since their parents were killed in an automobile accident. At the time Cara was barely twenty-one, Meg and Mark twelve and thirteen, respectively. The bond between the three was irrevocable. "Have you got complaints?"

"Not a one." Meg stood behind Cara's chair and massaged her sister's knotted shoulder muscles. "But what happens when we leave the nest? When you're on your own—all alone—wondering where your life went, where all the good men went."

"Oh, I oughta have a couple of years left to find someone after I get rid of you two, thank you very much. That is, if there actually are any 'good men' out there."

"That experience with Don has given you an attitude," Meg scolded, abandoning the massage and circling the sofa to sit by Cara. "Just because *he* let you down doesn't mean—"

"Learning Don's true nature was traumatic," Cara said, "and an experience I don't care to repeat."

From the day she'd met Don Axton, Cara had deferred to him totally. Don loved running the show and she'd followed his every dictate, catered to his every whim. Then when she'd desperately needed him to lean on, he'd suffered a meltdown like a hailstone after a summer storm. But he'd left behind a new doctrine for Cara. Never again would she abdicate control of her life. And if she ever allowed a guy to get close, it would be one she could depend on to stick around.

"But if you don't open yourself up, take some risks..." Meg was obviously intent on continuing her gloomy forecast for Cara's fate—the fate Cara could expect unless she took action now.

Meg was a smart girl, an honors student majoring in Textiles and Apparel, her eventual goal to design under her own label of high-fashion clothing. But despite the brains and ambition, Meg was also given to flights of fancy. Time for Cara to rein her in. "Enough discussion of my love life—"

"What love life?" her sister persisted. "If you don't watch out, that ship will have sailed without you."

"Great. According to you, now I've got two things to fret about—the auction and my dull, dreary future. Thanks a lot. I think I'll go console myself with food. Have you all eaten?" Cara rose and started toward the kitchen, her brother and sister tagging along.

They were almost through their tuna casserole when Meg leaned forward on her elbows, her eyebrows—blond and arched like Cara's—now pinched together. "We've got to figure out a new strategy."

"Strategy for what?" Cara asked warily.

"For snagging the Great McCauley, of course."

Cara sighed. If there was any subject less appealing at suppertime than a lost love, it was Wyatt McCauley.

"I'm pretty sure he jogs at Town Lake every morning. My friend Ginger has seen him there two or three times. She likes to follow him, to watch his moves. Says he has great buns, says—"

"Meg, is there a point to this?"

"Oh, yeah…well, tomorrow's Saturday, see. You could get there before he arrives and sort of accidentally on purpose run into him, then—"

"I'd like to run into him," Mark broke in. "Hard. Then when he's lying on his back, let him know how difficult he's making it for Cara with her boss."

Cara smiled. "Thanks, guys, but I don't think either method of running into him would help my cause."

"Mine might," Meg said, refusing to give up on her idea. "He'll be on an exercise high, in a great mood, you'll ask him again and—kaboom!—he'll consent."

"I can't imagine anyone getting in a good mood by working up a sweat." Cara hated exercise. As far as she was concerned, workouts—the fewer the better—were to be endured the same as spinach or broccoli on the dinner plate. Just because something was good for you didn't make it palatable. "I have no desire to mix with that throng of physical fitness buffs at Town Lake," she said. "Especially on the first Saturday in weeks when I don't have to work. I prefer to use my day off for something useful—like sleeping late."

"Listen to yourself," Meg scolded. "Preferring sleeping to meeting guys. I've met some *fine*—"

"Meg!" Cara's hand signaled "stop." "First, Wyatt McCauley's a business project, not a potential romance. Second, he's my problem to solve, not yours. You've got your own concerns to deal

with...like school. That reminds me—when are mid-
terms scheduled?''

''You sure know how to kill a conversation,'' Mark
groaned, then he and Meg began filling Cara in on
their course activities.

The meal over, Meg and Mark were studying and
Cara was washing the dinner dishes when the telephone rang.

''Well?''

The caller was Brooke. The one-word question—
and the fact Brooke was phoning from Dallas just
hours after Cara had seen her off from the Austin
airport—spoke volumes. Cara might be able to quiet
Mark and Meg on the subject of Wyatt McCauley,
but she wasn't about to silence her boss. Like it or
not, Cara had to try, try again.

Meg's informant had been correct. Less than a
hundred yards away, chugging toward her, was
McCauley—head erect, body balanced, intense and
wide awake. Cara couldn't say the same thing for herself. She stifled an emerging yawn and pretended to
stretch her muscles as she surreptitiously watched his
advance. The closer he got, the better he looked.

He was dressed in a gray T-shirt and skimpy gray
running shorts, his legs tanned and well-proportioned.
The man's body was as perfect as his face.

Self-consciously Cara stared down at her own bare
legs, which seldom saw the sun, thanks to long work
hours. True, there was no cellulite...yet, but the color

was a hospital white. *Why should I care how I look? This isn't about me.* Yet Cara had begun to feel as though it was.

Resisting an urge to trip the man for yesterday's upbraiding, Cara trotted up beside him, praying she could maintain the pace long enough to pitch the auction again.

Without breaking stride, he gave her a surprised flick of the eye. "Well, hello, Ms. Breedon. Fancy meeting you here."

The edge in his tone wasn't unexpected. "I happened to spy you jogging my way...decided to see if you've reconsidered helping us out."

"I did help—two checks, remember?"

"Your presence would aid even more," she said in a slightly breathy voice.

"No can do. Sorry." He sped up.

She sped up, too, determined not to lose him. "Are you sure?" Her voice was now jagged.

"Positive."

"Can't I—" pant, pant "—say anything to change your mind?"

"I think you've said it all. Might as well give it up."

"I—" gasp "—can't take—" another gasp "—no for an answer."

He glanced over at her, then began slowing before stopping altogether. "Oh, for heaven's sake, sit down before you collapse."

Gratefully Cara dropped onto the grass. She took

in great gulps of air and mopped her brow with a soggy tissue from her pocket. She guessed her face to be the shade of a boiled lobster from the physical exertion. After only a brief jog, her clothes were plastered to her body, wild strands of hair escaping from her ponytail.

It wasn't fair that, even sweaty, he still looked wonderful. The damp T-shirt clinging to his chest only emphasized his pectoral muscles and washboard torso.

Wyatt pulled a terry-cloth towel from his waistband to dry his face and neck, leaned against a tree to do a couple of calf stretches, then flopped down beside her, trying to come to terms with the rush of exhilaration he'd felt on seeing Cara. Every time he thought he'd brushed off the woman, she was back, as relentless as gum stuck to the bottom of his shoe. So why in Hades should he be secretly glad to see her? Anyone with the brains of a gnat would be seizing the advantage of superior conditioning and making a getaway. *But not you, McCauley—you blew it.* Well, he'd simply have to use other means to discourage her from this ceaseless pursuit.

He waited until Cara's breathing had settled then took her hand. "Listen, sweet cakes..." Cara yanked the hand away, but not before Wyatt's fingertips had memorized the softness of her skin.

So she objects to being called "sweet cakes." Wyatt smiled. *Or is it the touch she objects to?*

He had to admit that she was cute, especially now, all warm and rosy-cheeked. Those tender feelings were resurfacing. Whatever he tried to tell himself, part of him didn't want to get rid of Cara Breedon. Part of him... He stole a peek at her again and felt the temptation to smooth back one of those wayward wisps of golden hair.

Seeming to read his thoughts, Cara brushed at the unruly hair herself. As she did, Wyatt couldn't help noticing—no wedding ring. Cara Breedon was not only cute, she was available. *Cool it, McCauley. You're growing soft in the head. The lady's marital status is irrelevant. Remember her mission.* He should be taking steps to stop this paparazzi-like hounding. Since plain talk and directness didn't seem to work, maybe it was time for a different approach, a little reverse psychology.

Wyatt took Cara's hand again and held it. When she tried to pull away, he held tighter. "Don't be standoffish," he chided. "You've caught my attention like you wanted, so tell me about yourself."

"There's nothing to tell."

Still holding on to her, he lay back, pulling her down beside him. "Oh, don't be so modest. Surely there is. Who's the real Cara Breedon?"

She quickly sat up and scooted a few feet away. "No one important."

"Ah, but important enough to have wormed her way into my life." He sat up and moved nearer, resting his chin on her shoulder.

"Are you going to do the auction or not?" Cara blurted.

"I might be tempted…with the proper incentive." He grinned knowingly and, cupping her chin, pulled it toward him, his eyes growing smoky as his lips edged closer.

Cara jerked back.

"Don't act so coy," he drawled, the eyes now twinkling. "After all, you've been after me for weeks."

Was he serious or simply toying with her? Cara disliking both scenarios, shifted farther away, drawing Wyatt's laughter.

"I hope you're having fun," she huffed.

"That I am."

"Well, fun or not, I don't appreciate your conduct one bit."

"Maybe I merely wanted to see how far you'd go to please your boss…" Wyatt let the taunt hang in the air. He was still smiling.

"Believe me, not *that* far," Cara answered, staggering to her feet. Oh, what she'd give to swipe away that cocky grin of his.

"Well, if you have a change of heart—"

"You don't quit, do you?"

"Something we have in common."

"It's the only thing." Cara staggered off as fast as her wobbly legs could manage, feeling Wyatt's eyes on her every inch of the trek to the parking lot. She crawled into her car and slammed the door. "That does it! I'm through with that…that exasperating man. Nothing'll make me have anything more to do with him. Not even Brooke threatening me with insubordination.'' Cara continued the ranting all the way home.

True to her word, Cara remained steadfast against Brooke's nudges all week, each time telling her, ''It's no use.'' If it was to be a choice between appeasing Brooke or enduring another minute with McCauley, then Brooke's happiness would have to be sacrificed.

''You know I'm not free to handle this myself,'' Brooke complained. ''Am I going to have to assign it to someone else?''

The moment of reckoning was at hand. ''I suppose you are,'' Cara answered evenly. ''He's resisted every single overture. My bag of tricks is empty.'' Cara was not about to reveal Wyatt's unseemly proposition.

''But everyone's tied up on the new project,'' Brooke argued, unwilling to accept Cara's throwing in the towel.

Cara shrugged.

''The programs *must* go to the printer,'' Brooke whined.

''Absolutely,'' Cara said. ''The auction's only two weeks from tomorrow.''

''We still ought to compile a bio, prepare some publicity on Wyatt, in case he relents.''

''He's not going to.''

Steadfast or not, Cara's patience with the subject had run its course. She'd love to have a punching bag with Wyatt McCauley's image on it. And a dartboard with Brooke's. The two of them had made her a wreck. One as overbearing as a rottweiler and the other as tenacious as a rat terrier.

Brooke would probably still be hammering away about Wyatt the night of the auction. But at least she'd finally yielded to the reality that the programs couldn't wait. They would be at the printer's first thing Friday morning.

On the way home that afternoon, Cara picked up her brother and sister from the university library, then stopped at Central Market for groceries. As she pulled into the parking space, Mark and Meg spotted a group of friends on the patio of the market restaurant and scurried to join them, leaving Cara to shop alone. She was weighing tomatoes when she felt a tap on her shoulder. She turned around.

"We meet again." It was Wyatt McCauley. "I've missed you," he said. "Almost a week and no contact."

"I'm sure you've been waiting with bated breath." She set the tomatoes in her shopping cart and began examining the bell peppers, doing her darnedest to ignore the man hovering over her.

He picked up a large pepper and held it out to her. "This looks like a good one."

"I like these better." Rejecting the proffered pepper, she bagged two others and moved to weigh them. Wyatt was right beside her.

"Trying to snare another bachelor for the auction with a home-cooked meal?"

Cara rolled her eyes and pushed her shopping cart away. Wyatt trailed behind her. "Are you a good cook?" he asked.

Stopping the cart, Cara glared at him. "Now what are you up to?"

"Nothing sinister. Just trying to learn more about you." Wyatt's expression was the picture of innocence. "As I said before, you've captured my attention. Surely you don't mind my tagging along while you shop."

"But I do mind, so stop it," she hissed.

"No fun when you're the one pursued instead of the pursuer, hmm?"

"Is that what this is all about? Revenge for my bothering you? Then I apologize. I most humbly apologize. Now leave me alone."

"Have dinner with me."

"As you can see, I already have dinner plans." Cara gestured at her half-filled shopping cart.

"Change them."

"I can't."

"Some starved guy waiting for you to fix his favorite meal?"

"Matter of fact, there is." *My brother.* Mark was a bottomless pit, always hungry. Thank goodness he and Meg were occupied right now. She wanted no spectators at this ridiculous scene.

"Is he someone special?" There was pure seduction in Wyatt's voice.

"What's it to you?"

"Just sizing up the competition."

"Competition? Believe me, there's no competition."

"That's nice to know."

"Hold it. Let me make myself crystal clear. There is no competition because you are not in the running for anything involving me. Besides, you'll never convince me you're really on the level." Cara selected three chicken breasts and waited for the butcher to wrap them.

"It might be fun trying." Wyatt draped an arm around her shoulder.

"What's with you?" Cara asked, shrugging free. "Friday you were brusque, Saturday offensive, and now, now... Your behavior is definitely worsening." She pointed toward a nearby store employee. "Do I need to ask for protection against more harassment?"

"Oh, I see," he said with a knowing nod. "Okay for me to be harassed—at work no less, but when the tables are turned, the lady's ready to scream 'stalker.' Is that how it goes?"

"I've already apologized for bothering you. What else can I do?"

"Have dinner with me. If not tonight, then tomorrow."

She held her palms up. "Look. I explained that—"

"Tsk, tsk. What would your employer think? Passing up a golden opportunity to boost the auction again? A chance to lobby for your cause all evening."

"And what good would it do? You'd still say 'no.' Or attach strings. As far as I'm concerned, your refusal to participate is final and I have no intention of asking you again. Goodbye, Mr. McCauley.''

"Surely not goodbye." He gazed deeply into her eyes.

It was all Cara could do not to melt into a puddle at his feet. Wyatt McCauley seemed to inspire sappy behavior. "I've got to be going."

"When will I see you again?"

"How about never?" She rolled her cart toward the front of the store.

Wyatt watched Cara push up to a checkout lane, braking the urge to follow. Wandering over to the coffee bins, he tried to figure out why the woman intrigued him so. She'd been nothing but a grade-A irritation, so why had he even approached her tonight, much less invited her to dinner? He'd only stopped at Central Market for coffee beans, milk and fresh fruit. But then he'd glimpsed Cara and his senses had gone haywire.

Foolish of him abetting her shenanigans on behalf of the bachelor auction. He was asking for trouble by stirring her up. She might start a new recruiting drive... Wyatt shook his head. He didn't really believe that. Everything about Cara said she had washed her hands of him.

He'd like to change her attitude. His earlier words weren't simply a line. He *had* missed her. There was something about Cara that commanded his thoughts, excited him. And Wyatt hadn't been excited by a woman in a long, long time.

CHAPTER THREE

WYATT tore off a page of the yellow lined tablet he'd been doodling on and wadded it up, tossing the paper in a perfect arc toward the wastebasket where it joined a pile of other crushed missiles on the floor. At that moment Frances strode in and stopped, noting the empty wastebasket and its wreath of paper discards. "Busy today, I see. And your aim is rotten."

"Did you come in here for a purpose or to criticize my throwing skills?"

"Grumpy, too." She sat down in Wyatt's armchair and eyed him.

He caught her gaze. "I'm not grumpy," he said testily.

"What, then? You've been distracted all morning. Is something wrong?"

"No, nothing." He remained silent for a minute. "Is there any reason I should feel guilty about refusing to be part of that circus?"

"What circus?"

"The bachelor auction."

Frances studied him more closely. "No reason at all."

"Right."

"But you do?"

36

"Yeah. I suppose I do."

"Because of Cara Breedon?"

"What makes you come up with a crazy idea like that?" He didn't give Frances a chance to answer. "The Rosemund Center is providing a service to kids who wouldn't have a chance in life without—"

"I'm sure the center is pleased to welcome you as an advocate and benefactor. Only that's not what we're talking about, is it?"

Wyatt smiled ruefully. Frances could read him all too well. Still, he refused to rise to the bait. "Donations aren't everything," he continued. "Giving one's time is important, too. The auction also provides good publicity for the center. *That's* why I feel guilty."

"Of course it is."

"Even though I find the idea distasteful, the fact is, I could spare a couple of evenings if I felt like it."

"True."

"Well, you're a big help. You're supposed to tell me not to sweat it, assure me I'm too busy...blah, blah, blah, and get me off the hook. Now you've made it worse. Some assistant you are."

Frances laughed. "So fire me."

"Don't tempt me." Wyatt glanced at his watch. "Listen, tell Kenneth he may have to handle that staff meeting this afternoon. I'll be out of the office for a while...don't know when I'll get back." He reached for his jacket on the back of the chair. "See you later."

Despite his sermonizing to Frances about needy

causes, Wyatt didn't deceive himself any more than he had her. His remorse today didn't bear an ounce of altruism. Oh, the Rosemund Center was a worthwhile project, all right, but he couldn't care less about joining in the auction. What he did care about, he realized, was knowing Cara Breedon better. And the cursed auction seemed to be the only way to accomplish that.

Cara read the spreadsheet on her computer screen. "Ah, it tallies," she told herself. So engrossed was she in the financial report before her that when a hand from out of nowhere tapped her on the shoulder, she jumped, kicking the plug from the computer and causing the screen to go blank.

"Oh, no!" Wheeling around, she was even more shocked and annoyed to discover Wyatt McCauley behind her. "Do you make a habit of sneaking up on people like that?" she lashed out. "This is the second time you've done it, and this time you scared me half to death. Just look what you made me do!" She pointed toward the screen. "All my work…gone."

"Sorry. Was it something important?"

"Of course it was important!" she said, gesturing wildly. "What did you think? That I was playing computer solitaire?" Cara picked up a stack of papers and shook them at him. "Now I have to do it over."

"Surely you've been saving your work as you go along."

She knew what he was thinking. Anyone familiar with computers learned quickly and painfully about the perils of not backing up work, and actually, all but these last entries had been saved. She was torn over whether to appear the dunce or admit that most of the report could easily be retrieved. Unfortunately she couldn't have it both ways. "I'll still have to do some of it over," she complained.

"But not too much, I hope. Forget the report for now. Grab your purse and let's go. Since you weren't free for dinner last night, I've come to take you to lunch."

"I see." If McCauley thought this dictatorial stance would get him anywhere, he had another think coming. And Cara was about to tell him so except that one glance into those penetrating brown eyes almost made her reach for her purse as directed. But then she regained her equanimity.

Wyatt wasn't really here for a lunch date with her. He was a successful businessman with demands on his time. Probably happened to be in the vicinity and decided to enjoy a second round of evening the score. "I don't believe for an instant," she added, "that you drove halfway across Austin to—"

Her buzzing intercom interrupted. "The report?" Brooke prompted.

"Will be ready in about thirty minutes." *If you and the rest of the world will leave me alone.* Cara didn't need Brooke's nagging right now. Wyatt was enough to deal with... A satisfied grin appeared on her lips as a brainstorm popped into her head. She would divert Brooke's attention and teach McCauley a thing or two at the same time.

"It's just that Mr. McCauley is here," she said into the intercom, "and—" As anticipated, Brooke clicked off and came rushing out of her office, a look of elation on her face.

"Wyatt, as I live and breathe!"

"Hello, Brooke. I came by to take Cara to lunch. To discuss the auction."

A frown threatened to form between Brooke's eyebrows before she rallied. "Then I'm the one you need to be having lunch with, silly. I *am* the chairman, after all."

"Ms. Abbott's right," Cara agreed. "She's the one you should be talking to about the auction." She smiled sweetly at Wyatt as Brooke entwined an arm through his and pulled Wyatt toward her office.

"We can talk better here than in some noisy restaurant," Brooke cooed as she ushered him through the door. "Excuse me just a sec." She darted back to Cara. "Be a dear...call Marcel's and order lunch. Oh, and postpone this afternoon's session with the layout people until three."

Step into my parlor... Cara thought with diabolical pleasure as she reached for her telephone.

Revenge was taking its toll. For the past hour and a half, Cara'd been an unwilling party to Brooke's twitter and Wyatt's laughter, and she was sick of it. She'd delayed her own lunch to complete the report, re-schedule Brooke's afternoon agenda and handle an emergency call, so she was not only put out, she was starving, too. Her stomach growled, underscoring her hunger pangs.

At two-thirty the pair finally emerged from Brooke's office, Brooke wrapped around Wyatt like a love-struck anaconda. They came over to Cara's desk. "Mr. McCauley has graciously consented to be part of the bachelor auction," Brooke announced with un-concealed relish.

Cara, startled, looked up into Wyatt's face. "He has?"

"And not just a simple evening, either," Brooke gushed. "Wyatt's date will have the pleasure of flying with him to New Orleans for an overnight stay."

"How wonderful," Cara said, hoping Wyatt could read the mockery in her tone.

"Isn't it? This will be the highlight of the eve-ning," Brooke enthused. "I wouldn't be surprised if the bids top ten thousand, maybe twenty."

What woman in her right mind would waste all that hard-earned cash just to spend a few hours with a brash, know-it-all like Wyatt McCauley? Cara asked herself, then heaved a sigh. Any woman who could afford it, that's who. A woman like Brooke who was probably planning her travel wardrobe at this very moment.

"Oh, give Mr. McCauley our fax number," Brooke said, "so his secretary can transmit the details."

Dutifully, Cara grabbed a red pen, circled a number on one of Brooke's business cards and held it out for Wyatt. When he walked over to pick it up, Cara heard him say under his breath, ''I can hardly wait,'' before he moved away.

That was strange. He'd been so adamant with his refusals. Surely a couple of hours with Brooke couldn't have generated such a dramatic turnaround. Yet apparently it had. His previous ''no'' was now a ''yes'' and that megawatt smile beaming down on Brooke didn't indicate a man who was anything but delighted to be a part of her auction.

He *had* to know Brooke's ulterior motives. It didn't take a genius to figure out the woman, and although a major aggravation, Wyatt was no fool. Then again, maybe he *wanted* Brooke as his date. Maybe that was why he'd not only agreed to the auction, but had expanded the prize from a single date into an entire weekend. From all appearances, Wyatt was as taken with Brooke as she was with him. *So what do I care? I don't.* But watching the twosome grin like actors in a toothpaste commercial, Cara couldn't help wishing something would foil their little plot for a romantic interlude in the name of charity. *Charity indeed.*

Cara removed the papers from her printer and turned it off. She needed to get out of here, her rumbling stomach providing the perfect excuse. ''Here's the report. I'm off to lunch now,'' she told Brooke.

''Wait up,'' Wyatt called after her, ''and I'll ride

down with you." He kissed Brooke on the cheek. "See you at the auction."

"Not sooner?" Brooke purred.

"We wouldn't want anyone to think us in collusion—now would we?" His wink brought another broad smile from Brooke.

"I suppose you're right," she said almost with a giggle. Cara couldn't believe her eyes and ears. Brooke, a tough-nut businesswoman, was simpering like a teenager.

Cara waited as Wyatt had instructed, mumbled, "Thank you," when he opened the door to the hallway, then proceeded on her own toward the elevator, taking out her frustrations on the "down" button.

"Why so grim? I thought you'd be happy I'd decided to help you out." He pulled Cara's hand away before she could jab the button a fifth time.

"You aren't helping *me*. All you've done is make me look inept in front of my boss. She got a job done that I couldn't handle. You told *her* yes, not me. But I suppose it will benefit the Rosemund children. Someone's bound to fork over substantial bucks for the pleasure of your company." *And we both know who.*

"Someone like you?" he asked as they stepped onto the elevator.

"Hardly."

"You are going to attend the auction, aren't you?"

"Sure. But I'll be there to work, not to bid."

"You don't know what you'll be missing. It'll be

a memorable date. Dinner at Commander's Palace, a cruise on the Mississippi by moonlight. Sure you don't want to make an offer?''

"Is this more retaliation—making me spell it out in black and white? For your information I could no more compete in that auction than I could buy out General Motors.''

"Jeez, you're a sorehead when you're hungry.'' Wyatt took her arm as they reached the ground floor. "Let's get some lunch.''

"You had lunch.''

"I'll have dessert.''

"You had that, too. I ordered from Marcel's, remember?''

"I could squeeze in another one. An extra lap at Town Lake will work it off.''

"Look, I know I should be grateful you're doing the auction—and I am. But I don't want to have lunch with you. OK?''

"OK,'' he said agreeably. "I'll give you a reprieve—this time. See you at the auction.''

"You are stunning,'' Meg pronounced. It was the night of the auction, and she was fluttering around Cara, admiring her own handiwork. Meg had insisted Cara wear one of the cocktail dresses she'd designed for a recent competition.

Even if her oldest sibling couldn't afford the valet parking at the hotel, much less a thousand-plus dollars bid on one of the bachelors, she'd easily blend in with the horde of dressed-to-kill women scheduled to attend. "Good advertising for me," Meg said, but Cara intuited another motive—proving that Big Sis could indeed look like date bait.

The black halter-style bodice bared both Cara's shoulders and almost all of her spine inasmuch as it plunged to the waist at the back. The gown's red skirt flared out in tiered ruffles, giving the costume a Spanish look. For a finishing touch Meg pinned her sister's blond hair up and fashioned a small Spanish fan at the crown.

"There," Meg said. "Fantastic!"

Cara studied her reflection. "It's sorta far out, don't you think? All that's missing is a rose between my teeth."

"Get real, Cara. For once you're showing the world what a real glamour gal you can be. That clotheshorse Brooke will be so jealous."

"Brooke has other things on her mind. She'll be too preoccupied with her quarry to pay notice to anyone else."

"How much moolah do you think she'll ante up to ensure Wyatt leaves on her arm?"

"Whatever it takes. She will not be denied this opportunity. She's been lusting after him for eons."

Meg sat on the side of the bed. "Wouldn't it be nice to have money enough to buy a fancy date like that?"

"Actually it'd be nice to have money enough for new tires." *Money.* It had defined much of their existence the past seven years. "One of these days," Cara assured Meg, "when you're a famous designer and I'm a senior executive...maybe I'll buy myself a man, too. After the new tires, of course."

"If you keep looking like you do tonight, you won't need the green stuff to get the likes of Wyatt McCauley."

Cara did a pirouette in front of the mirror. "I am kind of snazzy, aren't I? Broke or not, I'll be one of the few women there wearing an original. And I'm going to let everyone know it's a Meg Breedon creation."

She gathered up her bag and car keys. "I'll be home early," she promised. "Filled with regrets at all the wonderful men who got away, and ready to cheer myself up with a pint of Blue Bell Dutch Chocolate ice cream."

The Driskell Hotel ballroom was aflutter with excited, chattering women, the din only slightly lower than that of its frequent political gatherings. On arriving, Cara was immediately dispatched by Brooke to inspect the flower arrangements. Bouquets of shasta daisies, lilies, and ivy in flowerpots served as centerpieces on the white-clothed tables and standing baskets of stephanotis flanked the stage, their heady scent battling with those of the guests' perfumes.

After assuring a harried Brooke that the flowers were perfect, Cara was sent forth on another mission, then another. Once every task had been completed, and knowing there was nothing more she could do, Cara looked for a corner to hide in. It was time for the festivities to begin. At a table near the back of the room, she found an empty seat which provided a dim-lit vista of the activities, breathing a sigh of relief as the lights lowered slightly and Brooke took her place at the podium as master of ceremonies.

Her earlier nervousness eased, or at least well hidden, Brooke did a commendable job of introducing each bachelor to the crowd. The tuxedo-clad male would ascend a few steps to a short runway, walk toward the audience, turn around, and pause under a spotlight while Brooke gave a brief biography.

Then Brooke would call for the submission of written bids to be quickly surveyed by a trio of board members. Brooke would be handed an envelope containing the winner's name and bid amount, which she opened and announced to the room. Even though there were loud oohs and aahs and a smattering of squeals after each announcement, the gathering was seemly and in keeping with its charitable purpose.

The first group of twenty men had been spoken for when an intermission was declared. Cara went backstage to see if Brooke needed anything and—amazingly—was told no. Hurrying away before a chore could be conjured up, Cara was dismayed to find herself on a collision course with Wyatt who was making use of the wait to place calls on his cellular phone. Hoping he didn't see her, she veered off at an angle. Too late.

He ended the conversation and came her way, studying her with unmistakable approval. "You look beautiful. Every guy in the place is going to be praying you win him. Except me, of course."

"Did you just compliment and insult me in the same sentence?"

"Not at all. I excluded myself from the prayerful because you said you couldn't afford me. Did you get all dolled up just to watch the bidding on me? I'm touched. Especially when *you* could have had a date for free."

"Actually I was considering bidding…a dollar seemed a good estimation of your value. Then again… Who knows? I might win. Decided it wasn't worth the risk."

"Ouch." He gave a good-natured chuckle. "So a dollar's all I'm worth, huh? Well, I only hope the rest of those ladies out front don't share your assessment."

"Not to worry," she said. "Some eager female will shell out big bucks for your company." *And I'm sure you won't fall over in a faint when Brooke announces her own name.* "Well, I'd better get going. The second half's about to start and you'll soon be on."

Intermission over, the auction resumed. Despite her limited role in the event, Cara found herself caught up in the excitement of the evening. The gala might be a tad frivolous, but it was bringing in loads of money, and besides, it was fun.

Yet when time came for the last participant, Cara's

mood took a decided plunge, catching her by surprise. Wyatt McCauley, for weeks a thorn in her side, was about to be removed, yet that knowledge didn't please her as much as it should have. There was something about Wyatt. Something annoying, she reminded herself. The reminder didn't help.

What is it? Do you hate imagining Wyatt with Brooke? Or with anyone? Do you want him for yourself? Nonsense. She didn't want him. And even if she did, so much the worse for her. Men like Wyatt McCauley didn't take everyday working girls seriously. Actually—from everything she'd read in the newspapers and heard about town—Wyatt didn't take *any* woman seriously. His girlfriends were tossed out like the pages of a calendar. New month, new lady. Not at all Cara's idea of Mr. Wonderful. Her dream man had to have staying power.

"I won't go into specifics about the marvelous weekend our next bachelor has planned," Brooke intoned, "since it's all outlined in the program. New Orleans, the French Quarter, Bourbon Street... Even a romantic boat cruise down the Mississippi River. Step up, Wyatt McCauley!"

Wyatt's turn down the runway would have done a fashion model proud, Cara thought. He was the only man she'd ever met who did more for a tuxedo than the tux did for him. Remembering their conversation about the purple underwear, she realized he didn't need to remove his clothes to look dishy.

What would it be like to actually be in the bidding,

to win? At the thought of New Orleans and Wyatt, Cara felt a prickly warmth permeate her body and she picked up the program to fan herself. When Wyatt's gaze met hers, she fanned even faster, chagrined at her thoughts and distressed that he had spied her fanning furiously. The only thing more vexing would be his knowing *why* she was all hot and bothered.

An usher handed the basket of bids to the board members seated at a side table and they immediately began their review.

"While we're waiting, a recap of a dream date." Brooke again recited Wyatt's plans for the weekend. "And just think, the lucky woman is to be off tomorrow morning. I hope she's a fast packer," Brooke twittered as the final envelope of the evening was brought her way.

She tapped it against the wooden podium, then held it up to the light, laughing softly. "Since you're probably all chewing off your nail polish wondering if you've placed the top bid, let's get on with it and end the suspense." She tore open the seal and pulled out a card.

"And, now for our final bid, for a fabulous weekend in New Orleans with Wyatt McCauley." Brooke looked at the card expectantly. She read it, did a double take, then read it again.

Cara had to give Brooke credit for an Oscar-caliber performance. Some first-rate acting was taking place here. To the unjaundiced eye it appeared that...oh, goodness, Brooke had forgotten she'd submitted a bid herself. Brooke gulped, a good touch Cara thought.

"Our winning bid for Wyatt McCauley is one hundred..." Another gulp. "One hundred thousand dollars."

A collective gasp filled the room.

"The winning bidder." Brooke's eyes were wintry as she stared into the audience, searching for the right face. The winning bidder," she continued, in a voice as cold as her eyes, "...Cara Breedon."

CHAPTER FOUR

THE sexy party dress exchanged for jeans and an old, oversize shirt, Cara sat in the wooden swing on her porch, castigating herself. Why hadn't she stood her ground in the Driskill ballroom tonight instead of running out of the hotel like she'd just robbed the place?

She'd done nothing wrong—if anything, she was the *victim* here, not the culpable party. If only she'd stayed to explain that there had been a mistake, that she hadn't placed a bid, that... Surely Brooke, at least, would believe her. Brooke knew Cara's salary. A hundred thousand dollars—why it would take her more than three years to earn that much. And the same amount of time to spend every penny of it on essentials.

This was Wyatt McCauley's doing. He was the only one with the means to pull a stunt of such magnitude. How he'd managed to tamper with the bidding, Cara was clueless, but she hadn't a shred of doubt that he was the culprit. A dark Mercedes pulling up in front of the house drew her attention. As the dome light framed Wyatt in silhouette, she mumbled, "Speak of the devil," to Snowflake who was curled up in her lap. She should have known that the car could belong to no one but him. Brooke drove a white

52

Cadillac, and friends of the Breedon family were strictly in the economy car category.

He was probably here to have one last laugh at her expense. "How did you find me?" she asked as Wyatt ambled up the walk.

"Pumpkin pieces littering the lawn, fat mice scampering about..." He gestured around the yard dramatically. "The glass slipper still hasn't turned up though."

"Very amusing," she said dryly. "And you must be Prince Charming."

"If the shoe fits...hey, I like that." He beamed with self-satisfaction.

"You're really on a roll, aren't you? Stop before I double over in laughter." Cara displayed the same taut mask she'd worn since his arrival.

His attempts at humor falling flat, Wyatt said, "OK, no more jokes. How did I locate you? You're the only C. Breedon in the telephone directory. Not too difficult." He sat down beside her on the swing, lifting her feet into his lap without comment.

Cara sat upright, yanking her feet away. "That's how—now *why* did you come here? Surely the shock waves haven't died down yet. I'm surprised you're not still at the hotel reveling in your little joke."

"There was no joke. You won me fair and square."

Cara's eyes rolled. "Fair and square my Aunt Fanny. *I* didn't win you because I didn't bid—but you did, in my name. There was nothing fair in any sense of the word about this little hoax of yours."

"You certainly know how to stomp on a man's ego, Ms. Breedon. Most women would consider getting me a triumph, and not go looking gift horses in the mouth."

"There are a lot of gullible women around," Cara grumped.

"Thanks a lot," he said.

"How did you pull it off anyway?"

"Well, Frances helped out."

"I find that hard to believe. She seemed too sensible for such pranks."

"At first she gave me hell, but eventually she came around. The Rosemund Center will be delighted with that big bank draft you—that is, Frances in your stead—enclosed in the bid envelope, confident it would be the highest offer."

"I'm surprised you didn't think you were worth a million. But I suppose that's too steep a price even for someone with your money. Still, you deliberately rigged the bidding—why?"

"To get you to go out with me, of course."

"Even if it meant committing fraud?"

"Fraud?" Wyatt rocked a hand back and forth. "Technically maybe...legally, highly doubtful. But who cares? The important thing is that the center is getting a huge donation and scads of free publicity. Everyone comes out ahead."

Cara gave him a sideways glance. "Not quite everyone. What about the women who bid on you?" *What about Brooke?*

"The bidding was a game of chance. No one was given any guarantees."

He picked up the cat and started stroking its back. The traitorous animal. Flake, as Snowflake was generally called, hated strangers, but she was arching and purring as though Wyatt McCauley were a plate of premium tuna.

"*Brooke* believed she had a guarantee," Cara reminded him. "Now there's an idea," she said with a snap of her fingers. "I'm going to call Brooke and give you to her."

"Lots of luck. How do you plan to justify outbidding everyone and then casually handing your date over to Brooke?"

"Shouldn't I be able to do whatever I want with my ill-gotten gains? Even use them to ingratiate myself with my boss?"

Wyatt shrugged noncommittally, then frowned. "But I don't want to go out with Brooke. She's not my type."

And I am? "You should have considered that possibility before you led her on," Cara said without sympathy, moving from the swing to the porch railing.

"Led her on? I had exactly one meeting with the woman. And you're the person who instigated it."

"Well, that one meeting should have told you she had her sights set on you. All that gushing and fawning in her office."

"I attributed the blarney and kissing up to her

thinking I'd help the auction and make her look good. That's the impression she gave me over lunch.''

"Looking good is one thing. Getting a date with you, something else entirely. And she expected to win a date with Wyatt McCauley tonight. Instead she was outmaneuvered by a lowly secretary—*her* lowly secretary.''

"Well, tough cookies. I can't help that. For gosh sakes," Wyatt continued, "she was the auction chairman, the one in charge. In my opinion, someone in that position shouldn't be in on the bidding at all— for me or anyone else." He shrugged. "So Brooksie's a bit peeved tonight—she'll get over it.''

"Don't be so sure." Cara had worked for Brooke long enough to know she didn't recover from a snit too easily. "Besides, Brooke committed no ethical faux pas. All the committee bigwigs were encouraged to bid for the good of the cause. I suspect Brooke's mad as hell. Maybe mad enough to can me.''

"Come on now. You're exaggerating. No way would she give you the heave-ho. It's not as if tonight were company business. She can't let you go simply because the auction didn't turn out the way she scripted it.''

"Brooke *owns* the agency. She can do anything she pleases, fire anyone she chooses. If you're aware of some law that says otherwise, I'd appreciate knowing about it. The only job protections I'm familiar with concern discrimination. And I hardly think my stealing her thunder falls into that category.''

Wyatt's brow creased in concentration as he weighed Cara's words and considered the impact of what he'd done. Several factors had prompted his manipulation of the auction results. First, he'd devoted entirely too many hours being preoccupied about Cara and had concluded that more time in her company would be a cure for that affliction. It had worked with every other woman he'd met.

Second, such an over-the-top donation wasn't likely to be matched or exceeded anytime soon, if ever. He should be off the hook for all future auctions, thus ending the hounding he'd endured from zealous board types in the past. With an unusual lack of foresight, however, he hadn't considered the consequences for Cara. "No, Brooke would never kick you out," he repeated, as much for his own benefit as to reassure Cara.

"I'm worried she will," Cara said glowering at Wyatt. "This date with you was important to Brooke. Then *you* go and sabotage her plans. And not because you really want to go out with me. All you want is payback for my pestering you. Well, you've got it. In spades. But, mister, all your high jinks went for naught, because I'm not going on any date with you."

Wyatt leaned forward in the swing. "Oh, yes, you are. That's the deal you pitched. I agreed to arrange a date and to parade around for that crowd of females. In return I supposedly got someone to go along on that date—the someone who submitted the winning

bid. So forget trying to palm Brooke off on me. We—
you and I—are off to New Orleans tomorrow.''

"And if I refuse?''

"What would become of the auction if the bachelors refused the date because they were dissatisfied
with the person who won them?''

"That's different.''

"How so? Because only the women can change
their minds? What's fair for the goose would have to
be fair for the gander.'' He wanted Cara's company,
darn it, but she sure wasn't making it easy. "Anyway,
think of the possible repercussions for the Rosemund
Center if people rashly started backing out. The fall-
out could sully the auction's reputation. There might
even be litigation.''

"Considering what you've done, I wouldn't even
mention lawsuits.''

"I was only speaking hypothetically. I didn't say *I*
intended to sue if you don't come on the date with
me. Although I suppose I could claim breach of contract.''

"Enough!'' Cara threw her hands in the air in ex-
asperation. Wyatt was obviously prepared to argue till
doomsday. "You win...I'll go on the damn date.''

"Your enthusiasm's touching.''

"If you want enthusiasm, call Brooke. I said I'd
go. I didn't say I'd like it.''

"Oh, but you will.'' He smiled, his brown eyes
twinkling. Wyatt rose from the swing and came over

to Cara, propping his arm above her on the supporting post and leaning toward her. "And since you've agreed to go, will you stop being such a spoilsport about it? I'll pick you up at ten, and we're going to have a great time...promise." He bent lower and kissed her, a soft, gentle kiss. It was as brief and as fleeting as a butterfly's touch, but it packed a wallop. As she watched him descend the porch steps, Cara realized that anxieties and bad feelings aside, the prospect of spending the weekend with Wyatt McCauley wasn't all that horrible.

"This is so exciting!" Meg ripped a faded, well-worn nightshirt out of Cara's luggage and substituted a lacy teddy.

Cara grabbed the nightshirt from Meg's hand and tossed the teddy on the dresser. "For heaven's sake, Meg, give it a rest. I'm not planning to sleep with the guy."

"Damn right," Mark chimed in, his tone parental, eerily like their father's.

"Cool it, Mark," Meg countered. "Cara's old enough to decide who she wants to sleep with."

"Who asked you, Miss Buttinski?"

"Look who's talking."

Cara put her hands to her ears and gave a mock scream. "Out, both of you." She pointed toward the door of her bedroom. "I don't need your advice or your squabbling."

Mark left as directed, but Meg lingered. "I didn't

mean to upset you, Cara. But you say you have to go...you might as well make the best of it. If Wyatt McCauley can afford to spend a hundred grand, then a few more dollars wining and dining you won't put a dent in his wallet. You haven't had a vacation in years so why not blow off all worries for the weekend and—"

"I can't blow off Brooke, my job. I'm worried sick. I'm surprised she hasn't already called and lowered the ax."

"Aren't you the one always telling us that worry doesn't accomplish anything? It's time to practice what you preach."

Mark wandered back in, a bag of Doritos in his hand. He offered the bag to his sisters. Cara shook her head. Meg sniffed the contents of the bag longingly, then pushed it away. "How can you eat so much and never gain an ounce?" she grumped.

Mark ignored her. "By the way, Cara, I heard what Meg said to you and she's right. Put away your troubles with Brooke till Monday. This is the first chance you've had for a real vacation. Take advantage of it. But be sure and keep some pepper spray handy in case McCauley—" A bell ringing interrupted Mark and eliminated further commentary from the pair.

"I'll get the door," Meg trilled, running off.

Cara shut the lid of her suitcase and snapped the lock. Mark picked up the bag, and as though anticipating an admonishment from Cara, told her, "Don't say it—I'll remember my manners. But McCauley'd better remember *his* this weekend, too.''

An hour later Cara was ensconced in one of the soft leather seats of Wyatt's private jet, sipping a mimosa and nibbling smoked almonds provided by a flight attendant. ''So this is how the other half lives,'' she said to Wyatt, returning his salute with the glass.

''Not usually, but I thought you might enjoy being pampered for a change.''

''Trying to get back in my good graces?''

''*Back* in?'' Wyatt's eyebrows arched. ''When have I come close to occupying that hallowed position?''

''Well, a few more sips of mimosa and I may forget that you're at the top of my enemies list.''

''Let's hear it for mimosas. So, are you glad you agreed to come?''

''Did I have a choice?''

''Then you're simply a martyr to the cause, giving your all for the Rosemund Center?''

''Oh, no, I may be an ardent new recruit for the center but not to that extent.'' *Especially if my all means what I think it means.*

Wyatt chuckled. He had gotten the message. ''Let me freshen that drink,'' he said, unperturbed at her pointed declaration. ''Since it seems to be the only thing I've got going for me.''

''That's enough for the moment.'' Cara pulled her

glass away. "I can see I need to keep my wits about me until I'm safe at home again."

Cara had been to New Orleans only once before, right after high school graduation, but she fondly remembered the old city with its rich history. Minutes after the jet landed, a limousine whisked the couple downtown to the Royal Sonesta Hotel in the heart of the French Quarter. She felt the same thrill she had as a teenager.

Wyatt gave her thirty minutes to freshen up and unpack, then tapped on the door of her room, which was across the hall from his. "I thought we'd walk down Bourbon Street, maybe duck over to the Court of the Two Sisters for lunch and some jazz, then check out the sidewalk artists at Jackson Square. Does that sound OK?"

Cara nodded and draped her camera around her neck. "I should be able to get some good pictures."

As they walked the short distance to the restaurant, Cara felt comforted to discover that the French Quarter had not undergone a massive change. There were still many points of interest that looked precisely as they had ten years ago.

After dining on an assortment of local specialties— crawfish étouffee, shrimp with remoulade sauce, dirty rice—Cara and Wyatt were dawdling over a decadent dessert of pecan pie, accompanied by cups of rich chicory coffee. "I feel like I'm storing up for winter hibernation." Cara put down her fork. "That is delicious, but I can't manage another bite."

"A shame to let pie so good go to waste. Guess I'll have to make the sacrifice and eat yours too."

"My hero." She handed him her plate.

Wyatt smiled and accepted the pie. "I always make a point of coming here," he said, "for the atmosphere as much as for the food. Did you enjoy it? Do you like the jazz?"

Wyatt was being the perfect gentlemen, the solicitous host, but Cara was not adjusting quickly to this change in tempo. Expensive junkets and leisure time were as alien to her as shopping without a budget. Too, she didn't like being in the dark as to where she stood. She was still reeling over that preposterous bid. And while one part of her couldn't squelch a giddy elation that Wyatt'd made such an outlandish gesture, another more sensible part refused to believe he'd go to such lengths simply to snag a date with her.

She looked into his face and realized he was waiting for an answer to his question. "Yes, I love this place and the jazz, too. In fact, I enjoy— Why are you doing this?" she blurted, unable to hold her tongue any longer.

"Doing what? Eating dessert?"

"Don't be obtuse. Explain to me what's happening here."

He glanced around the restaurant. "I don't see anything out of the ordinary. I'm a man and you're a woman, a desirable woman I'm trying my best to impress. That's what's happening here."

"Oh? Well, it defies logic. Why me? Originally I

chalked it up to getting even, but no one would go this far.''

"So what's wrong with the obvious reason—me escorting a beautiful lady who happens to stir my senses?''

"That's flattering, but about as plausible as Brooke phoning New Orleans to say she hopes we're having a good time. I hear the talk and read the society columns. The women you squire around aren't ordinary working girls like me—they're debutantes, actresses, heiresses. And apparently a different one every week. You seem to attract more females than Brad Pitt.''

"Quite true," Wyatt agreed with a grin, "if you discount the kazillion women who wouldn't miss one of his movies.''

"Well, one on one, I bet you'd best him. Still, I'm hardly in a position to verify the facts since I don't run in your *or* Brad's circles. But I'm not naive enough to think this *date* is because you're so taken with me.''

"You are a stubborn gal, that's for sure, and you don't give yourself much credit. You got my attention the first time I ever saw you. Even if you were hidden behind all those roses." He took her hand. "You must admit that spending a hundred grand does indicate a teensy bit of interest.''

"So, you're sincere?" she said, pulling the hand away. "I really am the McCauley flavor of the month?''

"Now that's just plain insulting—to both of us." His dark eyes flashed with indignation.

But Cara wasn't contrite. "Admit it...your reputation isn't exactly saintly. Love 'em and leave 'em is more your style. You're not the type for engagement rings or wedding bells."

"Is that what you're after, Cara—rings and bells, commitment, marriage?"

"No...well, someday. Right now, all I want is to help my brother and sister finish their educations. Everything else is on hold until that happens."

"Unless you land a rich husband in the mean—" Wyatt stopped, wanting to muzzle himself for persisting with this subject. Cara just might get the wrong impression, think he really was contemplating a future for them. He wasn't looking to the future at all—with Cara or any other woman. Divorce had cured Wyatt of such susceptibilities. As a born-again bachelor, he saw marriage as an institution riddled with negatives.

For the present, he was merely indulging himself with Cara. An indulgence that would end as soon as he'd banished her from his nightly dreams.

Cara broke into his thoughts. "If you're volunteering, then thanks, but no thanks. I've got enough problems without having to deal with Austin's own Mr. Fickle."

"Man, you really are heartless today. And you accuse *me* of trying to even the score. At the moment you're way ahead in the retaliation department." Her continued rejection got to him, even though all logic told Wyatt he'd bolt like a startled wildebeest if he thought Cara *did* want to marry him. "What problems were you referring to before?" he asked, deciding it was definitely time to change the subject.

"My job. Remember?"

"Oh, that."

"Yes, that."

"So what's the worst that could happen if your dire predictions come true and Brooke does lower the boom?"

"Starvation, homelessness...well, not really. But it could be rough going. You are aware, aren't you, that plebeians like myself exist from paycheck to paycheck? Or have you lost touch with the common folk?"

"You tell me. Enlighten me as to how it is with you proletarian types."

"Not now—too boring and depressing. We're supposed to be vacationing. I thought you were going to introduce me to the sidewalk artists."

"OK, but first things first." Wyatt signaled to a waiter and asked him to take a picture for them. The shot of her and Wyatt seated on the restaurant's patio, Wyatt's arm draped around her shoulders, was one Cara knew Meg the romantic would love. No matter that the scene was a sham.

"Thank you," she told the waiter as he returned the camera.

Leaving the restaurant, they strolled toward Jackson Square. Even though the frolics of pre-Lenten Mardi

Gras were weeks past, a bevy of tourists still mingled in the streets. At the square, Wyatt insisted on purchasing a set of small watercolors for Cara. "A souvenir of our trip," he said.

She started to protest, then stopped. The artist was talented, yet unknown, hence the paintings were inexpensive. Not worth quibbling about a modest gift with a man who threw thousands around. She would give the paintings a prominent spot at home where she could relive the sights and resurrect memories.

"Now let's go take in the river," Wyatt said. By the time they finished sight-seeing along the embankment and browsing in some of the shops, it was nearing six. Wyatt reached for a cell phone and within minutes, a limo pulled up.

Doesn't the guy ever hail a cab like regular people? Besides, they were only four or five blocks away from the hotel. They could have walked. Each new extravagance jolted Cara back to reality and reminded her how different their lifestyles were. Once they were inside the limo, Wyatt said, "Dinner, then a river cruise. I made reservations at Commander's Palace, but I can cancel them if you've got somewhere else in mind." He rattled off the names of several exclusive restaurants.

"Truth?"

"Anywhere you'd like."

"After that big lunch, I'd rather save Commander's Palace for tomorrow. Could we just go for a shrimp po'boy tonight?"

"You're sure?"

"Positive. My dad brought me here years ago, just the two of us, as a high school graduation present. It was a wonderful trip. And one of the memories that's stayed with me, believe it or not, was the po'boy...the crusty baguette piled high with fried shrimp. I've never had another to match it. Nothing sounds better to me right now."

Wyatt touched his fingertips to his forehead like a genie responding to his master. "Your wish is my command. I know just the place." They detoured by the hotel, changed into jeans and T-shirts, then drove north toward Metairie, stopping at a takeout seafood shop. "I discovered this hole-in-the-wall a few years ago," Wyatt said, handing her a paper bag. "Now we need to find a site to do these sandwiches justice." He reached for his cellular phone. "If you don't mind skipping the river cruise, I have a friend with a sailboat," Wyatt explained. "I only need to make a quick call."

A few minutes later the limousine dropped them at a yacht club on Lake Ponchartrain. After stopping at the gatehouse for keys, they made their way down a long pier and boarded the last in a row of sleek boats. "Do you want to go out on the lake or just stay here and watch the moon and stars?"

"Why not just stay moored? The view's beautiful," she said, staring at the eastern horizon and the huge moon that hung in the sky there.

"Not nearly so beautiful as you." Wyatt turned her

face to his and his lips gently grazed hers. "Very nice," he said, pulling back to gaze into her eyes.

"Nice," Cara repeated, her voice almost a croak. "But…maybe we ought to eat before our sandwiches get cold." *And before things between us get any hotter.*

"Whatever you say." Wyatt disappeared below and returned with a bottle of champagne and two stemmed glasses. Cara knew she couldn't have created a more romantic setting if she'd had the poetic talent of a Browning or the artistic skill of a Raphael. Maybe she had misjudged Wyatt. Maybe he *did* really like her. After all, he'd done everything possible to make today special.

During the meal, they shared histories, Wyatt telling her how he'd conceived and developed his computer business and helping her understand that his wealth had only begun accruing in the past few years. His upbringing was strictly middle-class, the same as hers.

By the time the meal was over and the champagne bottle empty, Cara was feeling decidedly mellow. Her qualms about being a McCauley fling were forgotten for now. The moon had moved directly over them and was bathing everything in a romantic glow, so romantic that when Wyatt wrapped an arm around her, Cara didn't even flinch. When he started nuzzling her neck, however, the caution lights came on.

Bringing her watch closer to her face, she said,

"It's getting late." She rose and began gathering glasses and refuse. "Where can we deposit these?"

"I'll show you." Wyatt took her hand. "And I'll give you a tour of this craft before we go."

Below was a galley, a small sitting area and a separate room. Wyatt swung open the door to reveal a bedroom, a seductive bedroom. There was a tiny nightstand with built-in controls for an elaborate music system now vibrating with the soft sounds of a Spanish guitar, an inviting bed piled with pillows, dim lighting. "I take it your friend is a bachelor."

"Why do you say that?"

"Well, for one thing, he stocks champagne. Plus these make-out quarters..." Cara glanced up. "I'm surprised the ceiling isn't mirrored."

"What do you know about mirrored ceilings?" Wyatt propped a hand against the doorjamb and gazed down at her.

"Only what I've read in books."

"Oh, and what kind of books would those be?"

"I'm not going to get into that kind of discussion with you," Cara said. "We need to go."

"Nervous?"

"Tired." *And nervous, too.*

"OK, we'll go, but not before I do this." He leaned toward her, trapping her between his body and the wall.

He bent his head to hers and his mouth settled on her slightly parted lips. Maybe the champagne was working overtime, but Cara offered no resistance. On the contrary, her arms wrapped around him and her fingers pressed against the firm muscles of his back. The soft kisses were a thing of the past as Wyatt hungrily pressed his mouth to hers, his breath heavy on her cheek.

As he finally released her, Cara couldn't stifle a sigh. Gentle or demanding, Wyatt's kisses were heavenly. Was it the craft's motion or her own reaction that caused her to go all wobbly and weak in the knees? She was afraid of the answer.

Wyatt nuzzled her ear, whispering, "If we're leaving, I think we'd better make it now."

"We're leaving," she said, thankful for the narrow escape.

CHAPTER FIVE

ON SUNDAY morning Cara and Wyatt had brunch in the upstairs Garden Room at Commander's Palace. "I've always wanted to eat here," she said, savoring a last bite of bread pudding soufflé. "The French Quarter is wonderful, but this is my favorite section of New Orleans."

Wyatt reached for her hand. "Lake Ponchartrain's now mine."

Cara pulled her hand away, refusing to respond to Wyatt's attempts at intimacy. Last night was...well, last night, and in the clear light of day she had to keep reminding herself not to get too wound up in a world of make-believe. Wyatt might be romancing her in style this weekend, but if old habits won out, soon there would be another flavor of the month.

"Well, Lake Ponchartrain's nice, but I still like it here—the nearby universities, the streetcars rumbling by the old homes along St. Charles Avenue, Anne Rice's house..."

"You sound like you're auditioning for the local Chamber of Commerce. Shall we check and see if they have any positions open?"

Cara wanted to shoot back with yes, she might just be in need of a job, but held her tongue. Why spoil a lovely meal with grim reminders about the future? "What's next on today's agenda?" she asked.

"The zoo. Is that OK with you?"

Cara touched his arm, surprised that Wyatt would choose such a commonplace activity. "I love zoos."

"Me, too." Wyatt smiled, and those brown eyes were as welcoming as hot fudge syrup.

Two hours later they were strolling arm in arm around Audubon Zoo, pausing on benches to rest and talk, and Cara was thoroughly enjoying herself. With every passing moment, she felt less tense. This eager-to-please Wyatt was so far removed from the egotistical swine she'd envisioned being stuck with all weekend.

Despite the fact he'd forced this trip and his company on her, she found him more and more irresistible. He was entertaining, considerate...

Careful, Cara, you're succumbing to that fabled McCauley charm. Maybe. But it sure felt good.

Wyatt sat on a bench, arms spread across the top, and watched as Cara took pictures of some dozing alligators. She called to them, even talked baby talk to the cumbersome creatures in hopes of catching their eye and capturing the perfect shot. The alligators, however, were indifferent to her efforts and continued to laze in the shade, barely moving a muscle and showing nary a toothsome grin.

A little girl carrying a yellow helium-filled balloon raced up beside her and Cara bent to chat with the child, slowing her progress until the youngster's parents could catch up. Wyatt watched as Cara took the balloon and tied it loosely around the tot's wrist, then made the little girl feel oh-so-important by requesting that she and her family pose for a photograph.

For a second Wyatt tilted his head up to the sky, letting the sun hit on his face before he rested his eyes once more on Cara and her new-made friends. Most of the women he knew would have ignored the child, but not Cara. He felt a warmth that had nothing to do with the sun or the muggy New Orleans weather. Wyatt felt completely comfortable, at peace. The fact that he was happy, happier than he'd ever remembered, brought him up short. Instead of tiring of Cara's company the way he usually did with other dates, he'd simply grown more enchanted with her over the past two days.

She was gutsy, exuberant, honest...kind, pretty, sexy—and a great kisser. She'd hung tough through some difficult times. That, and the fact she was supporting her brother and sister through college, spoke volumes about her character.

Cara finished the picture taking and walked toward him. "Well, now that I'm out of film, those sloggy gators will probably start tap dancing." She pushed the rewind button on her camera.

Wyatt pulled her down beside him on the bench. "Here, have a soft drink and forget those rude reptiles. They don't deserve to be in your pictures."

Gratefully she took the paper cup. "Tastes good on a day like this."

Wyatt's face turned serious. "Tell me more about your parents." Suddenly he found himself wanting to know every detail about her. "It had to be a crushing blow, losing them both at once."

Cara tucked her camera into a tote bag. "It was a terrible loss. One day they were here, and then—in a flash—gone. Such a shock. Fortunately I had little time to feel sorry for myself. There was so much to do that grief could only be allowed in small doses.

"My dad was a self-employed construction worker and my mother a homemaker, so there wasn't any money or insurance to speak of. But we did have the house and I was only a few credit hours away from a degree, so I was able to go to work and knock off my remaining courses one by one.

"Meg and Mark pitched in by taking part-time jobs—baby-sitting, paper routes, fast-food service. That, combined with student loans, meant we could get by and hang on to the house till we got more solvent.

"Unfortunately I didn't get a chance to use that psychology degree I struggled to finish. The job market was tight and I didn't have the luxury of searching for employment that would enhance a career. I took the secretarial position with Brooke because it paid well and I hoped it would lead into something better with the firm."

"But it hasn't?"

She shook her head. "Brooke is happy with me as her secretary, said she couldn't stand to lose me as her right arm. Nice to be needed, but not exactly where I want to be for the rest of my life. Yet, she does pay well, and since I still have heavy financial obligations..." Cara sighed. "Of course this may all be moot now anyway."

Discussing Brooke brought back the nasty reminder that come Monday she'd have to deal with the woman. Unless a lot of cooling down had taken place since Friday, it wouldn't be an amicable encounter. Her boss would be wanting her head on a platter. The specter of Brooke's furious face haunted Cara's thoughts.

"I could help." Wyatt took her hand. "Let me take care of some of those obligations, any outstanding loans. Then later—"

"No, thank you," she interrupted. Cara wished she hadn't been such a blabbermouth. Talking with Wyatt had become so natural that she'd forgotten herself. He was a wealthy man, probably used to people hinting for his assistance, if not asking outright. She didn't want to be indebted to him that way—any way. "My family does not accept charity."

"Not charity, a loan. Give you some breathing room—"

"Until I paid it off, it would be a gift, a handout. I shouldn't have said anything." Clouds began to gather, the bright sunshine of the day now filtered through gray. Cara felt as though more than the weather had been affected. Her sunny mood had also darkened.

"Of course you should have said something," Wyatt protested. "Friends talk about their problems...we are friends now, aren't we?"

"I suppose we are," Cara answered. "And you know what they say, friends should never borrow money from friends."

"I botched that argument up, didn't I?"

"That you did. Maybe you meant well with your offer...just don't do it again." Her gaze was stern, then she patted his hand to soften the admonishment.

How she wished she'd never strayed into this conversation. Self-consciously she studied her surroundings. More for something to do than anything else, she looked at her watch. "It's after three."

Wyatt stood up. "Time to go, I guess." He bent and kissed her. "I like being with you, Cara Breedon."

Cara smiled, but didn't answer. Better she keep quiet or, in a fit of honesty, she might blurt, "I'm falling in love with you, Wyatt McCauley."

The drives to the hotel and then to the airport and the flight home passed entirely too quickly for Cara. By seven, she and Wyatt were in a limousine heading back toward her house. As if tying up the weekend with a bow, Wyatt pulled another bottle of champagne from the limo's minibar and offered Cara a glass.

She shook her head. "I think I've had more than enough to drink over the past two days," she said.

Wyatt insisted, "One last toast."

Cara took the glass and Wyatt clicked his against hers. "To winning grand prizes at auctions."

"*You*, naturally, being the grand prize?"

"I was thinking of *you* as the prize."

Cara rested her glass on the top of her leg without taking a sip. The intended compliment caught her off guard. Was that what she was—a prize, a trophy? Cara had gone to New Orleans loaded with trepidation about Wyatt and fears for her career. But during the magical hours together, she'd relaxed and exposed her heart.

She should have known better. How dumb to throw caution to the wind and allow herself to become enamored of a trained seducer. Now it was crystal clear that to Wyatt all the weekend meant was some sort of coup, attaining the unattainable, having the last word, the last "gotcha!"

The limousine rolled to a stop in front of her house. She and Wyatt climbed out and he waved the driver aside, carrying her luggage up the sidewalk to the front door himself. For seconds they locked eyes with one another, each searching for a way to say goodbye. He bent down to kiss her, and though she didn't turn away, Cara invested no emotion in the kiss.

"I don't know about my schedule for next week," he said, "but when I get a chance, I'll call—"

"Please don't. The weekend was nice...very nice. But all obligations...yours, mine...have been met. Why don't we just leave it at that? Thank you for the trip…the paintings…everything. Good night.'' She disappeared inside.

Wyatt stared dumbly at the closed door. He felt as though he'd been slapped. *Obligation?* Was that the extent of what these hours together meant to Cara? He'd swear some kind of fusion had taken place between them—he still felt the heat. So why not play it out, go with the flow until it ran its course? Apparently, Cara had felt no fusion. He walked back to the limousine and slumped inside, the glow from their date fading faster than holiday fireworks.

''Tell me all about it!'' Meg shrieked as she burst into Cara's room that evening where Cara was unpacking.

''Where's your brother?'' Cara asked, ignoring her sister's question.

''He'll be along later. We didn't expect you back so early.''

Cara flicked her eyes to the clock radio on the bedside table. ''Early? It's nine o'clock.''

Meg shook her head. ''Really, Cara, sometimes you amaze me. Adults actually stay out to ten, eleven, even midnight. Feel free to do so anytime you want.'' She sat on the bed and crossed her legs beneath her. ''So?''

''So it was a pleasant weekend and now it's over.'' Cara took some undies from her suitcase and tossed them in the clothes hamper.

''Pleasant? Over? How can that be?''

"What were you expecting, sweetie, an elopement?"

"No, not yet. But after all the hoopla, you two can't just drop it. People will be so disappointed."

"What people? What hoopla?"

"Hold on a sec." Meg scurried from the room and rushed back with a newspaper in her hands. "You and Wyatt are quite an item. Take a look at this story about the auction."

Cara could see a headline reading "Super Bid Rocks Austin." Adjacent was a picture of Wyatt taken during the auction proceedings and one of her shot a year ago at Lake Travis.

"Where did the newspaper get this photo of me?"

"I gave it to them."

"Why, for pity's sake?"

"Why not? This real nice reporter called to talk to you. When he discovered you'd already left for your trip, he asked if he could come out and get some background information from me and I said yes. Not only that," Meg said, her excitement growing, "Channel Seven called for an interview. And believe it or not, *Happenings* magazine!"

"Oh, no!"

"What's the matter, Cara? I thought you'd be impressed."

Cara ran a hand through her hair. "Meg, don't you realize what mayhem this can cause? Now I have to worry about losing my job *and* my privacy. There's going to be speculation galore. Everyone will wonder how a secretary came up with that much money. And me? I'm stuck for an explanation. Brooke will assume I'm taking bribes, that or selling drugs on the streets.''

''You could tell her and them the truth, that Wyatt made the bid in your name.''

''Exposing Wyatt's dirty tricks wouldn't benefit my cause…probably just make matters worse. The truth certainly won't make Brooke any happier—just the opposite. And I can imagine what the bidders would think about the fairness of the process. Especially those who bid for Wyatt. Once the word is out, the auction's integrity is compromised, supporters wary. The result could be a big drop in donations for the Rosemund Center. I can't let that happen. I'll just have to ride out the embarrassment and the suspicions. I could strangle Wyatt McCauley!''

''Darn. I was hoping for magic to happen in New Orleans. Imagining having *him* as a brother-in-law…'' Meg closed her eyes dreamily.

Cara frowned. Meg was always promoting, encouraging a romance for her big sister, even though Cara seldom dated. In this instance, however, she could understand Meg's whimsy. Cara herself had almost gotten caught up in a pipe dream about what might have been. And ever since Wyatt had left her at the front door, she'd been lecturing herself about her lapse in judgment.

Now the conversation with Meg had deepened her recriminations. Wyatt McCauley was trouble. She probably wouldn't have any problem remembering that in the future.

Cara spent most of that night stewing over the damage Wyatt had done to her reputation, to the extent that she'd let it overshadow her concerns about seeing Brooke the next morning.

Clearly she should have spared a minute or two for fretting about her boss. Brooke Abbott was on a rampage, summoning Cara into her office the instant she arrived at work. Brooke was breathing fire, her pretty face contorted in rage.

Cara's predictions about Brooke's vindictive reaction to Wyatt's maneuverings had come true. In spades. "I can't believe you would deliberately undermine me that way," Brooke ranted, pounding the desk for emphasis. "All this time I've been overpaying you and throwing bonuses your way...partly because I thought you needed the money."

Bonuses? The only bonuses Cara could recall were small monetary gifts at Christmastime. And everyone at Abbott got those.

"Obviously you had a tidy nest egg that I knew nothing about. You sure pulled the wool over my eyes with that fake frugality. Creepy old car, lots of sack lunches from home, clothes made by your sister..." Brooke cast a glance at Cara's tailored navy suit. "Nice, but still homemade."

Cara stared stonily as Brooke took a breath.

"What was it? A roll of the dice to land a rich husband?"

Cara opened her mouth to protest, but Brooke kept on. "You *knew* I was interested in Wyatt McCauley, knew that I'd been hoping for a date for months. But did that matter to you? No, you snuck around and betrayed me, rammed a knife in my back."

Brooke took an exaggerated breath. "So what do you have to say for yourself?"

Cara wanted to say something, anything, to explain. But what? There was no explanation except the truth, and the truth wouldn't serve anyone well.

"All I can say is I'm sorry," Cara said. "I've done nothing intentionally to hurt you."

Brooke emitted a brittle laugh. "Well, thank goodness it wasn't intentional. I'd hate to think what would have happened if you'd *meant* me harm. I'd probably be reduced to a pile of ash."

It took every smidgen of grit and determination for Cara to stay there, putting up with Brooke's abuse. If it hadn't been for her obligations to Mark and Meg, she would have quit on the spot. But she did have those obligations. She simply couldn't give up one job without another in the wings. So for now, groveling was the only avenue open and she took it, galling though it was to humble herself after Brooke's virulent attack. "Is there anything I can do to make it up to you?"

"Yes, I'll tell you exactly what you can do. Gather up your stuff and get out. There's no way I can deal with an employee I can't trust." She pointed to the door. "I'll give you fifteen minutes to pack up and go. A minute longer and I call security to have you thrown out. Your severance papers and final check will be mailed. I hope never to see your face again.''

Cara opened her mouth, closed it, then turned and trudged toward the door of Brooke's office. Quickly boxing her belongings and dumping them in her car, she headed straight to Wyatt's office, her anger and indignation mounting with every mile.

"I need to see your boss." This time she carried no flowers. Instead, what Cara bore was an all-consuming rage.

"Mr. McCauley's downstairs holding a meeting in the conference room," Frances said. "It should be over soon. Would you like to wait?" She gestured to a cluster of chairs in the small waiting area.

Cara plopped down in a chair and crossed her legs, jiggling her foot in agitation. She needed a shoulder to cry on about Brooke and Wyatt, but Frances would hardly do. After all, her loyalty was to Wyatt. "Holding a meeting?" Cara was surprised he wasn't out and about sweet talking another hapless female, some new conquest.

"May I get you some coffee, Ms. Breedon?"

"No, thank you," Cara said. Her stomach was churning—the last thing she needed was coffee upsetting it even more. Brooke's tirade played and replayed in her brain. *Overpaying*—boy did that rankle! Brooke paid well, true, but she was also demanding. Hour upon hour of overtime, lunches late or not at all, stress-inducing deadlines...and never an acknowledgement, an "atta-girl."

That "trust" comment really chapped her too, like Cara'd embezzled from the company or filched cash out of Brooke's wallet. Surely someone you'd worked for over six years could cut you some slack, rather than going ballistic. Not that it made any difference now, but never had Brooke proclaimed, "McCauley's mine. Touch him at your own risk." If she had, at least her case for betrayal would have more substance.

"Hello there." Wyatt stepped off the elevator and crossed over to her. "To what do I owe the pleasure of this visit?"

Cara's eyes shot sparks. *Believe me, it's going to be no pleasure.* But before Cara could give voice to her thoughts, Frances answered in her place.

"Wyatt, you've had three calls. All supposed emergencies." She passed him a trio of pink message slips.

Wyatt glanced at the slips, then at Cara's stormy expression. "Appears I've got a bigger emergency on my hands. Return the calls and tell them I'll get back to them as soon as possible." He opened the door to his office and stepped aside for Cara to enter.

"So what's with the look?" he said, dropping down on the couch and patting the seat next to him invitingly.

She didn't accept, but hovered menacingly over him, hands on hips. "This is the look of someone who's just been axed. Not very nicely, either. Because of *you* I lost my job."

Wyatt rose and reached for her, but Cara shrugged away. "What can I say? I'm sorry, Cara. I truly never thought—"

"I know that," Cara retorted. "You never thought." Wyatt had deceived himself into believing his mischief to be innocuous, but he needed to understand that he couldn't go around manipulating women willy-nilly without repercussions.

"Look, I'll make it right. I'll call Brooke, explain—"

"After this morning's conversation with that woman, I wouldn't work for her again if she offered me twice the money and half the duties. I've already humiliated myself trying to get back in her good graces. I wouldn't go back now if she crawled on her knees to my house and begged, if she—"

"Really rough, huh?"

"Rough probably would have been preferable in comparison. It was demeaning. She screamed loud enough to be heard in the next county. I was shocked and mortified."

"Then I don't blame you for refusing to go back to that kind of behavior. And you don't have to. I'll contact personnel and arrange a position here—one you've been wanting, with growth potential."

"There you go again with another of your handouts. I didn't come here to ask for help. You've helped quite enough already, thank you. Besides, getting me fired is only half of your mischief."

"And the other half?"

"The press. So far there have been calls from the newspaper, two television stations, and a couple of national magazines. One reporter even tried to talk to me as I was backing out of the driveway on my way to work."

"Jeez." Wyatt rubbed the back of his neck. "Some calls have come in here too, but I didn't know you were being harassed."

"Well, now you do. So how do you propose to fix that? Wave your wallet? Buy out the TV stations? I don't think you have enough money to finagle your way out of this one."

"I doubt that I do, but I've a connection or two. I'll—"

"I didn't come here to ask you to muzzle the media either," she snapped, cutting him off.

"Then why did you come, Cara? Just to tell me off? To launch me on a guilt trip?"

"I...I..." Cara was stumped for an answer. She wished like crazy that she hadn't come. That's what she got for letting her emotions get the best of her. Brooke had enraged her to the point that Cara had jumped in her car and driven like a maniac over to Wyatt's office building. She should have gone somewhere and counted to a thousand, to ten thousand. But she was so distraught, so mad at Wyatt for creating this sorry plight, that she wanted nothing so much as to confront him and let him know what he'd done to her life.

And how had he responded? An apology and then

a hasty attempt to fix what he'd messed up. *You're unemployed? No problem. I'll just give you a job with my company. Press bugging you? Leave it to me.*

Cara stared at Wyatt with dismay. Apparently this was his way of dealing with any problem. Using his money and power to make any necessary adjustments. Mr. Fixit. "I know you have this inherent need to dominate every situation, Wyatt. I even understand it. But it's time *you* understood I'm through being jacked around by you. I merely came to tell you to your face the outcome of your meddling. That done, I'm now going." She started toward the door, only to be stopped in midstride by Wyatt.

He grasped her shoulders and turned her around. "I got you into this, dammit, and I insist on doing something to rectify the damage."

"And I insist you stay out of my life. If I live to be a hundred, I never want to find myself in a situation where *you* are the one making decisions about my welfare. Goodbye, Mr. McCauley. Goodbye and good riddance."

CHAPTER SIX

AFTER her tirade at Wyatt's, Cara stopped by the Texas Employment Commission. Doing so wasn't an undertaking she relished, especially in her current mood, but she knew she could let no grass grow under her feet. She *had* to find work and if worse came to worst, explore unemployment benefits.

As she was studying the materials, a woman approached her. "Aren't you that secretary who won the guy in the auction Saturday?"

Eyeing her warily, Cara lied and said no.

The woman persisted, "Well you sure look a lot like her picture. For a second there, I thought maybe you'd spent all your money on him and had to take a second job." She laughed.

Cara laughed feebly along with her, then turned around and left before the woman could come up with any more painful observations.

Spent from what were now three upsetting confrontations, Cara pointed her car toward home. Once inside, she removed her business suit and slipped into an old sundress. Thank goodness Mark and Meg were on campus all day. It wasn't yet noon so she had hours in which to lick her wounds and weigh her fate before her brother and sister came home and she had to start making explanations.

A soothing cup of spiced tea in hand, she sat at the kitchen table with a notepad and the Sunday paper retrieved from the recycle bin. It had been years since she'd done any job hunting, so the first order of business would be checking out the expanded Sunday want ads, then dusting off and updating her résumé.

A quick survey of the Help Wanted pages showed nothing promising. A Hobson's choice between an entry level human services position with opportunity for advancement, or a couple of clerical positions that listed higher starting salaries, but still paid ten to twelve thousand a year less than she'd been earning with Brooke. "Beggars can't be choosers," Cara reminded herself, "and beggar is where you'll be very soon."

Starting over, she went back, examining each ad carefully and circling several. She'd work on her résumé this afternoon, then call about the jobs early tomorrow.

Pushing the notepad and classifieds aside, she sipped her tea and moved on to the rest of the newspaper, in particular the article Meg had waved in front of her face last evening.

Cara hadn't the stomach for reading the article then. Now wasn't any easier. She scanned a bit of the column, groaned and folded the paper over. Today had been devastating enough without subjecting herself to another rehash of Friday night.

*   *   *

"I can't believe that witch," Meg said on hearing Cara's bad news that evening.

"It's totally McCauley's fault," Mark growled. "This disaster has his name written all over it."

"Laying blame isn't going to accomplish anything," Cara chided, wondering why she bothered to protect Wyatt. The last thing the man needed was her rushing to his defense. Why, he'd probably recovered fully from the diatribe she'd delivered at his office and was focusing on his date for next weekend, with nary a thought to her dilemma.

Through dinner, the trio discussed ways to cut corners even further. "It looks like we have three choices," Mark said, holding up the same number of fingers. "One, accept the deal from that last tabloid that called—"

"Option one is out," Cara said.

"Figured you'd say that. Sure you don't want to rethink it? Would be easy money."

"Mark." Cara narrowed her gaze.

"OK, OK. Moving right along. Two may take a while to gel since it involves your landing a new job plus Meg and me bypassing summer school and finding something full-time for those three months."

"Forget that option, too." The siblings had already come up with a graduation plan, a plan which involved both youngsters picking up extra course credits during the summer.

"Or we can see about more student loans," Meg chimed in.

"That's option three," Mark said. He gave Cara a sly glance. "Since you won't go for the easy money, I think it's the best choice at the moment. Don't you?"

Cara sighed. Meg and Mark were already employed part-time on campus, as well as carrying heavy course loads. Plus, she'd vowed that the family wouldn't have to go deeper into debt to finance their educations. It appeared she was going to have to renege on that vow. "I feel terrible," she said.

"Forget it." Mark gave her neck an affectionate squeeze. "It's not like you had any control over the situation."

"Isn't that the truth," she told Mark. "I feel like I'm caught in a whirlwind frantically looking for something, anything to hang on to."

"Well, for sure you can hang on to us. But if I know my big sis, that won't be necessary. She'll ride that whirlwind like a rodeo champion on a bucking bronc. Be back on top before she knows it."

Cara understood that Mark was giving her a pep talk to boost her spirits, and she appreciated what he was attempting to do. Only he underestimated the uphill battle she faced. Just as well, she decided. No use all three Breedons turning into basket cases.

She would start job hunting in earnest tomorrow...check on those ads...call private employment agencies. Without quality references, however, it was going to be tough convincing would-be employers that she was a good hire. Most job applications asked for permission to contact previous supervisors, putting her in an untenable position. If she said yes, Brooke would sabotage any possibility of getting the job. If she said no, it would arouse suspicion as to why.

Following her brother's lead, Meg, too, was intent on bolstering her older sister's spirits. She cooked her speciality—white lasagna—and cleaned the kitchen afterward. Both young people stayed home rather than joining friends at Starbucks. Cara told them to go on out, but they refused. "You've always been there for us...we want to be around when you need support."

The three were watching a television sitcom, Meg and Mark monitoring the telephone, which had rung a half dozen times. Five of the six calls were the media; the sixth, Wyatt McCauley. "Listen, McCauley," Mark began, obviously ready to deliver a few well-chosen words.

Cara quickly intervened, giving Mark a fierce frown. "Just say goodbye," she commanded.

"Goodbye!" he barked obediently.

During the commercial Mark escaped to the kitchen, returning with a package of Oreos and glasses of milk for all.

"I may be out of a job but I'm counting my blessings anyway," Cara said, lifting her milk in a toast. "We have each other—we can face the world."

"Here, here," said Mark.

"And a pox on Brooke," Meg joined in.

"Here, here." They were clinking glasses when the telephone rang again. This time Meg answered. It was eight o'clock and she'd been promised a call at that hour from a new boyfriend.

"Meg, I need to talk to your sister."

"She..." Meg looked to Cara for guidance, whispering, "It's *him* again."

"Oh, what's the use." Cara grabbed the receiver. "Why are you calling?"

"To make sure you're OK."

"I'm just dandy. And I'll continue to be if you leave me alone."

"This conversation is beginning to sound oddly familiar. Besides, you're the one who burst into my office today with tales of woe and finger-pointing in my direction."

"Well, it won't happen again. I was just getting something off my chest."

"And a helluva good job you did. You made me feel rotten about what's happened. Have breakfast with me tomorrow and let's talk—"

"Is it absolution you want?" Cara sniped. "I'm sorry, but I'm not ready to give it yet. Not on the phone, not at breakfast. Goodbye, Mr. McCauley." She hung up. The telephone rang again. "It's all yours, Meg," Cara told her sister. "And if it's McCauley again, I've left the premises."

For the next three days, Cara reacquainted herself with Austin's job market. It wasn't an altogether positive exercise. People were kind and courteous for the most part, but there was a serious gap in what she needed to earn and what was out there for an ex-secretary with an unused psychology degree. Brooke was extracting more blood than she'd realized. Then again, maybe she did realize.

By Thursday, desperation had Cara firmly in its grip. She'd come home from her latest interview, changed into shorts and T-shirt and was printing out more copies of her résumé when the telephone rang.

"Hi, Cara."

Wyatt again. He'd called every day and she'd either brushed him off or had Meg and Mark run interference for her. Today she said, "Look, haven't you done enough damage? Thanks to you, my life is in utter chaos...my career is down the drain, every reporter within a thousand-mile radius is bugging me.

"Between being fired, not being able to find another spot, and having every Tom, Dick and Harry with a camera trying to snap my picture...oh, please, just leave me alone." She hung up.

Wyatt placed his receiver in its cradle and pressed tented fingers against his lips. Man, he really had screwed things up for Cara. And even worse, she wouldn't let him do anything, wouldn't let him comfort her, show her he cared. Just the opposite—she was pushing him away.

Wyatt was brought up short by his own feelings. Why was he so concerned about her? It wasn't as if he had deep feelings for the woman, as if he...no, certainly not that, not love. But if it wasn't love he felt for Cara, what was it? Wyatt emitted a loud exhale. *I don't want to entertain such thoughts.*

He turned his head at the sound of Frances's tap at the door. "Come in."

Frances studied him. "You've been in a blue funk ever since Cara Breedon's visit on Monday. But right now you look glummer than you have all week, like you just finished sucking on a bushel of lemons."

"Do I need to install a dead bolt on my door to halt your daily put-downs?"

"And you're getting touchier by the minute." Frances moved in for closer scrutiny. "What's happened now that's moved you from merely blue to downright miserable? No, don't tell me. Let me take a wild guess—there's a new snag in the Wyatt-Cara story."

"There *is* no Wyatt-Cara story," he huffed. "Quit trying to make us into Romeo and Juliet."

"I know a lovesick mug when I see one. Someone's got it bad, really bad. So maybe not Romeo and Juliet, but Antony and Cleopatra, Dr. Zhivago and Lara, Charlie Brown and the little red-haired girl—"

"I hate to ruin your soap opera scenario, but I don't aspire to join the ranks of romantic couples. My one go-round as part of a duo was quite enough for me, thank you."

"My, oh, my, I wondered how long it would take you to bring that up. Poor Wyatt," she mocked. "His ex-wife has ruined him forever for other women." Frances eyed him critically. "Your marriage to Jocelyn ended years ago...that excuse for rotating the women in your life like a farmer rotates crops is getting a bit old.''

"Lessons like that stick with one a long time," Wyatt grumbled.

"Well, as they say, 'get over it.' Jocelyn and Cara are about as different as night and day and you know it. Now why not spare us a lot of sparring around and just tell ol' Frances what's happened with Cara to get you so on edge.''

"What's got me so on edge, you ask? Well, first I have an executive assistant who's prone to idle speculation and—''

Frances shook a finger at him. "Wyatt McCauley, quit dancing around the subject and tell me what's bothering you.''

Wyatt tilted in his chair, eyes focused upward. Frances was a jewel, but she considered it not only her right, but her duty, to pester him until she got at the truth. He might as well tell her and get it over with.

"I've caused problems for Cara…gotten her fired because of that bid—'' he held up a hand "—and not a word about how you warned me about it being a bad idea. I remember. Unfortunately, now it's a done deal.''

"So fix it.''

"She won't let me.''

"Since when does Wyatt McCauley get permission before he acts?''

He frowned. "Since never.''

She straightened up. "Need I say more...except to ask how you'd manage without me?"

"Yeah, yeah," Wyatt said. He waved a dismissing hand. "Now scram. I've got some calls to make." He reached for his telephone.

"Glenn," he said, "can you meet me for a drink later?" He then called Wade Hendrix, and after Wade, Cy Winslow. All three men owed him favors. One of them could damn well ride to the rescue.

Feeling pleased with the results of his job recruitment meeting with Glen, Wade, and Cy, Wyatt decided to go by Cara's. He stopped by a florist on the way and bought a mammoth bouquet of flowers, hoping the peace offering might win back some lost brownie points.

When he rang the doorbell, she answered, a government textbook in hand. "I was wondering how long it'd take you to remember—" She stopped in midsentence. "You!"

"Expecting someone else?"

"Mark. He's meeting with a study group. He forgot this." She lay the book on a nearby table, then stepped onto the porch. Wyatt needed to understand he wasn't welcome inside. In fact, she would do her best to get rid of him before Mark came back.

"These are for you." Wyatt held out the flowers to her.

Cara hesitated a moment before accepting the bouquet. She wanted to turn him away, but couldn't.

Irrational though it was, Cara surrendered to a surge of pleasure. She couldn't remember the last time a man had brought her flowers. "They're lovely. Thank you. And now you'd better go. My brother's not too high on you these days."

"I suppose I deserve his disapproval...but what about us? Isn't there some way to mend fences? Do we have to stay enemies forever?"

"I don't know. I'm not sure. I'll think about it."

"Promise?"

"Yes, if you'll just go." She looked past him to see if the approaching car was Mark's. Thankfully it wasn't.

"Anxious to be rid of me, aren't you?"

"Frankly, yes. And I've already told you why. Mark's not one to hold back his feelings and I'm not in the mood for any unpleasantness tonight."

"All right, I'll go. After you give me a goodnight kiss."

"No way."

He came a step closer. "Then I guess I'll just hang around. Find out what old Mark's up to these days."

"Oh...here." Cara leaned forward and planted a quick kiss on Wyatt's cheek. "Now go."

"You call that a kiss?"

"You didn't specify quality."

"I didn't know I needed to. Guess I gotta remind you what a real kiss is." In the blink of an eye, Wyatt wrapped an arm around her waist and whipped her against him, crushing her flat against his chest. Cara expected a comical demonstration. Instead it was a show of passion—a hand cradling her head, another pressing her tight to him, Wyatt's actions suggesting a hunger that ran much deeper than kisses. The stirrings she was experiencing told Cara how close her feelings paralleled his.

In what seemed too brief a time, Wyatt released her. It was so abrupt, she almost staggered backward.

"Now that's a kiss," he said. "See you." He bounded down the porch steps and made his way to his car.

Two hours later, Cara was sprawled on the sofa having fallen asleep in the middle of a television program. When the phone rang, she groggily fumbled with the receiver and tried to get her bearings. Awakening from a dream about Wyatt, she automatically answered, "Why are you calling now?"

"Hello?" a confused male voice said. "May I speak with Cara Breedon?"

Not Wyatt at all. "Um, this is Cara," she said cautiously.

"Jeff Mayo. You may not remember me, but we met at the Home Show last year. You were there with Brooke Abbott."

Cara rolled her eyes at the mention of Brooke's name. "Of course," Cara said, not remembering at all. "I apologize for sounding out of it, but I... uh...thought you were someone else."

"I should be the one apologizing for calling at night, but I was in a meeting that ran late. The reason

I phoned, Cara,'' he continued, ''is, word on the street says you're no longer with Brooke Abbott. Are the rumors true?''

Cara didn't like the direction this conversation was taking, especially in view of all the media interest. However, his knowing about the auction and having the particulars of the skirmish with Brooke were two different kettles of fish.

Was Mayo a reporter? Did he want some sort of comment from her? Too bad—he wasn't about to get one. On either subject. ''I'm sure you already have all the grisly details. Everyone else does.''

''Probably not all. Just what I've read in the papers.''

''Are you a journalist, Mr. Mayo?''

Unexpectedly he laughed. ''No way. But after the publicity you've gotten this week I can understand any caution on your part. Again, I need to say I'm sorry. I should have explained before. I'm personnel manager for Sweeney and Winslow Advertising and I'm recruiting for an account executive. You may not be aware of the fact that people in the business give you a lot of the credit for Brooke's recent successes. Secretary was hardly an adequate title for all the hats you wore over there.''

''That's...complimentary,'' Cara said, unsure exactly what was happening here.

''Well, the reason I'm calling is that I was hoping you hadn't signed on with anyone else yet. We'd like to talk with you before you make any commitment.''

"You mean, an interview?" Cara asked, unable to believe her good fortune. Sweeney and Winslow was one of the top firms in Austin.

"Yes. A position just opened up that seems tailor-made for you. We'd like to have you come in and discuss it."

"Well, OK," Cara said, dazed. *Was he for real?* Companies weren't exactly lining up to beg for her presence in their workforce. She hadn't even gotten a nibble from any of her applications. "Who exactly recommended me?"

"At lunch today I was meeting with some guys in the industry. One of them mentioned that Brooke had let you go."

"So I'm part of the local gossip mill," Cara responded, aggravated. What had Brooke done—issued a news release saying her secretary had been sacked?

"Actually it was more flattery than gossip. There was one hundred percent concurrence that Brooke made a dumb mistake—she'll quickly discover she can't find her way out of her own office without you."

"I know you're overstating the case to be nice, and I appreciate it," Cara quickly said, too much in need of a job to let false pride get in the way. "Anyway, I suppose gossip's the name of the game in the advertising business."

"All too true. And remember, as far as Brooke's concerned, your living well will be the best revenge."

Cara's antennae raised. "This isn't a competition thing, is it? Because I should say up front I won't be willing to go along with luring away any of Brooke's accounts or—''

''Whoa there. We may be competitors of Brooke's but I promise no one will be asking you to raid her client list or to reveal any of her methods. That's not why I sought you out. But I've got a position to fill. Are you interested or not?''

''Sorry,'' Cara said. ''I suppose I'm still reeling from the events of the past few days. All the publicity…plus losing my job.''

''That's completely understandable. So, do you still want that interview?''

''Yes, definitely.''

''Wonderful. Why don't you come in tomorrow at nine-thirty and we'll talk? Our office is on North Lamar.''

''Great. See you then. Thank you, Mr. Mayo. Thank you very much.'' Cara hung up the receiver and dropped back on the sofa, arms outspread. Just when she'd thought she was a goner, a call right out of the blue!

''You won't believe this,'' she said to Meg when her sister arrived home a few minutes later, ''but I've got an interview—for a *better* job than before.''

''All right!''

Mark entered the room. ''What's all right?''

After Cara repeated her good news, Mark said, ''We've got to do something to celebrate. Let's order in Chinese.''

''Fried wontons. Just what I need,'' Meg quipped.

"Forget your diet. This is a special occasion," he admonished. "Besides, some guys prefer women with meat on their ribs," he added, playfully pinching skin from his sister's midriff.

Meg, who was trim, but always gaining and losing the same five pounds, made a fist and aimed a mock swing at Mark. "One of these days, Mark, one of these days."

Cara was still in bed when the doorbell rang on Saturday morning. *Meg or Mark will get it.* When the bell persisted, she glanced over at the clock. "Ten-fifteen!" She must have been drained from the week of tension to sleep so late. They had gone to their Saturday jobs without waking her. She threw on a robe and went to the door.

"Well," Wyatt said. "Now I know why you refused to do breakfast—you're a closet slugabed. Do you know it's after ten?"

"I'm perfectly aware of the time, but what's that to you? And why are you here?"

"Crabby in the morning, huh? Well, I guess that's one of your faults I'll just have to put up with."

"Don't do me any favors," she grumbled. "You still haven't told me why you're here."

"I thought I'd come over and take you to early lunch since you vetoed breakfast the other day. After all, you're out of work because of me. No way can I allow you to starve."

Cara knew she should refuse, should stay as far

away from Wyatt McCauley as possible. However, after yesterday's successful interview at Sweeney and Winslow, she was no longer unemployed and she couldn't resist the opportunity to rub it in to Wyatt as to how she'd landed on her feet. "Well...I suppose that *is* the least you can do," she said, wanting him to think she was reluctantly acquiescing.

"Right," Wyatt answered good-humoredly. "Why don't you go make yourself presentable and I'll watch cartoons or something on TV. Unbidden, he came into the house before she had a chance to change her mind.

They selected a small restaurant off Thirty-eighth Street. During the drive there they talked of the weather, Meg's and Mark's activities, the recent kite-flying contest in Zilker Park, which Wyatt had participated in.

After they'd been seated at a small corner table, Cara smiled at him. "I still can't believe you entered a kite in the contest."

"I can't believe I didn't win," Wyatt said plaintively. "Actually I enter every year. My sister has a ten-year-old son and it's become a joint project of ours. Lily's divorced and Danny's father lives in Seattle so the kite contest is one way I can give him guy-time."

"Do you have other family in Austin?"

"No, our folks and two other sisters live in Corpus Christi."

"So you're the lone boy in the family," Cara mused. "That explains a lot."

"Oh? Sounds ominous. Care to go into detail?"

"Just that you're probably used to being catered to by females."

"Really, is that how you see it, Doctor Cara?"

"Uh-huh. You're probably a bit spoiled—"

He took her hand. "I don't think I want to hear any more. Besides, I'd rather talk about you."

"Talk about what?"

"Like why you're in a much better frame of mind today. It took me aback when you agreed to lunch without a big argument. I thought maybe you were plotting to use the occasion for slipping cyanide into my food."

She gazed up at him. "Now that you mention it," she teased, "there is a certain appeal in that idea. And after all that's happened, a jury would probably call it justifiable homicide."

His thumb was making little circles on the back of Cara's hand. "So tell me. Where is that glow on your face coming from?"

She'd never readily confess it, but part of the glow came from having a man with desirable deep brown eyes sitting across the table from her. Staying mad was impossible when her heart kept sending her different messages. Luckily the moment she'd been waiting for, the moment Cara had been saving her news for, had arrived.

"What you see in my expression is the happiness from having a job. As an account executive with Sweeney and Winslow."

Wyatt whistled. "They're bigger even than Abbott. How did this come about?" he asked innocently, knowing full well he'd pay a heavy penalty if Cara ever discovered the true answer to that question. His friend Cy—one of his Thursday night drinking buddies—was the Winslow part of the firm. Once Wyatt had shared Cara's plight, Cy had charged his personnel manager with the task of helping the damsel in distress.

Wyatt watched intently as Cara excitedly described the turn of events that'd led to her being hired by Sweeney and Winslow, animatedly describing the call and the interview. Maybe it was because he was tired of women who appeared eternally bored by the everyday or maybe it was because Cara... Wyatt paused, thoughts bouncing around in his brain. *Here I go again, mind growing mushy.* Something about Cara was getting to him.

Wyatt had come to view women as temporary distractions, not permanent fixtures in his life. He'd tried permanent with Jocelyn and it'd lasted a few measly months. To Wyatt, long-term no longer implied binding legal commitments like marriage, but rather having more than a half dozen dates with the same woman. That's about how long he lasted before it was time to move on. A low-risk, preemptive-strike approach to relationships.

Cara was intriguing because he hadn't yet reached that sixth-date cure. Who knew, with Cara he might have to devote more time than that, get past his arbitrary deadline, go to eight dates, even ten, before he could get her out of his system.

"Spend Saturday with me," he said, now tracing a fingertip across her knuckles.

"Two Saturdays in a row. Won't that ruin your love 'em and leave 'em reputation?" she deadpanned.

"I think my reputation will be enhanced. After all, I'll be going out with the new media darling."

She groaned. "I just may go home and pull down the shades."

"Are you still being hounded?"

"The past day or two has been better. Only a couple of calls. We may be losing the spotlight to that preacher in Abilene who was arrested for having four wives."

"A good scandal like that does tend to steal the show." Wyatt laughed. "I'm glad there's been a reprieve. Too bad you haven't had Frances running interference for you like I have. Now, back to Saturday." When he thought he saw a refusal forming, Wyatt added, "Just a casual day. We can visit the Wildflower Center, then grab a hamburger. Unless you'd like to do something more daring? There's always Hippie Hollow."

Cara laughed. "Not that daring." The swimming hole located near Zilker Park had a reputation for nude sunbathing. "And even if I were so inclined, don't you think it's a bit cool?" The April breezes were casting a slight chill on the day.

"I don't know. All that flesh can heat up a man's blood."

"Then let's keep your thermostat in control. The Wildflower Center it is."

As Cara lingered at her front door watching Wyatt drive away, she realized that she'd acted on impulse. She didn't plan on dating Wyatt McCauley. She'd only gone to lunch with him to gloat about her new job. Yet before they'd parted, she'd agreed to see him again.

What harm can it do, her impish side taunted. *The harm of a broken heart,* her sensible side responded.

CHAPTER SEVEN

ONLY a handful of cars dotted the parking lot of the Wildflower Center when Cara and Wyatt drove in. "We're in luck today," Wyatt said, "ahead of the crowds." He eased into a convenient spot and they climbed out of the car just as a flash went off.

"What was that?" Cara turned to see a photographer snapping their picture.

"Hey, buddy," Wyatt called. "Cut that out!"

"It's a free country."

"I don't care how free it is. Go bother someone else." Wyatt strode menacingly toward the photographer.

"Touch me, McCauley, and you'll be talking to a judge. I'm only trying to make a living. Kevin Costner was supposed to be filming here today. He's a no-show, and you're the subject by default. So don't get a big head, you're strictly second choice." He turned to Cara. "So tell me, little lady, where did all that money come from?"

"Somewhere more respectable than your source of income," Wyatt snarled. "Cara, get back in the car," he barked in her direction. "We're leaving." They sped from the parking lot, the squealing tires of

Wyatt's car punctuating his fury. He slapped the steering wheel. "Vultures."

"It's all right," she soothed. "There'll be another time for the wildflowers."

"The only thing that will make it all right with me is if you agree for us to go someplace else."

It was all too easy to say yes. Wyatt was good company, their time together special to her. Cara knew she was sinking in deeper with each encounter, but still, she couldn't resist the lure of being with him.

They drove into the hill country west of Austin, savoring the beautiful day, stopping for a scenic view of the Pedernales River, then on to Fredericksburg where they wandered around town, enjoying the German architecture and sampling local wurst.

Heading back to Austin, Wyatt suggested dinner at a restaurant near the university. Their drinks had just been served when a patron approached them with a camera.

"Aren't you the two from the auction?" she asked excitedly. Before either of them could formulate an answer, she continued. "Do you mind if I take a picture to show my friends?"

"Well…we, oh, go ahead," Wyatt said.

She aimed her camera and clicked. "Just one more in case that one didn't come out." She was aiming again when the restaurant manager intervened.

"I'm sorry, ma'am, I'm going to have to ask you to restrict your picture taking before you annoy the other diners."

"Of course," the woman said, looking slightly embarrassed. "Well...thank you." She scurried back to her own table.

The manager leaned in. "Sorry about that. If anyone else bothers you, just let me know."

"Thanks," Wyatt answered.

"Do you think they'll ever leave us alone?" Cara asked.

"Eventually." He took her hand. "I'm sorry if your day has been spoiled."

"It hasn't," Cara assured him. "Unless you're so upset by the attention you plan to take me home without feeding me."

"Not on your life. It's time for me to grow a tougher hide anyway." Wyatt signaled for a waiter. "So, the new job still going OK?" he asked once their orders had been taken.

"Fantastic. Working at Sweeney and Winslow is more satisfying than I could ever have imagined. I keep pinching myself to be sure it's not a dream. With Brooke I felt like a peon. Now I'm treated like a junior executive—and with my own secretary, no less.

"This is no dead-end job, but a real position with upward mobility. What I'd always hoped for with Brooke has finally become—" Cara stopped. It seemed so natural sharing her enthusiasm with Wyatt, but she was carrying on entirely too long. "What about you? What's going on at your office?"

He told her about a new contract he was pursuing, then they talked about Meg and Mark. The meal passed all too quickly and by eleven they were saying their goodbyes on Cara's front porch. Wyatt was flying to Tokyo the next day for a business trip. "I'll call you when I get back," he said, kissing her goodnight. The kiss was long and intense, Cara cocooned in his arms, she and Wyatt as closely entwined as two people could be.

"I'm getting too old for front porch kisses," Wyatt groaned, his lips nibbling provocatively at her ear.

"Me, too. Even though I feel I could stay out here in your arms forever." She ran her fingers down the back of his head and the nape of his neck, loving the feel of hair and skin.

"So why not more?"

"Too soon," she answered. Numerous undeniable sensations told her it wasn't in the least too soon, but Cara would not give an inch as long as the relationship remained tenuous. Her body hurt all over from the denial but it didn't hurt half as much as a broken heart—her broken heart—would. It already seemed that every time Wyatt left, he took a bit more of her with him. If she gave in to her desires, Cara doubted she could bear to be parted from him.

Although she realized the experience with Don had made her wary of involvement, Cara was only beginning to understand the extent it had colored her thinking. The simple truth was that before she could give in to her yearning for Wyatt, Cara needed some guarantee there would be a tomorrow for them. From what she knew of Wyatt, Cara couldn't picture him ever issuing such guarantees.

Wyatt returned to Austin the next Friday. He continued to ask Cara out and, despite her concerns, she continued to see him. Not that they dated often, only every other week or so. For one thing, work intervened—his and hers. He was busy traveling again, and she was putting in long hours trying to prove herself in her heady new job.

Besides, she knew firsthand there were other women. Not that he'd admitted as much, but she personally witnessed one of his dates on a Wednesday when he was entering Serrano's with a comely redhead just as she, Meg and Mark were backing out of their parking spot.

"Isn't that McCauley?" Mark asked, stopping the car to gawk.

"I'm not sure," Cara hedged, knowing full well it was Wyatt, his hand on the waist of some incredibly gorgeous woman, her mane of hair cascading past her shoulders.

Wyatt had a perfect right to date others, darn it, and Cara didn't want to endure a family discussion on the subject. Still she had to quell an urge to leap from the car, run over and pull out every strand of the woman's glorious red hair.

"I'd swear it was Wyatt," Mark insisted. "Didn't you see him, Meg?"

"No. I was searching the floor for my contact lens. Who was he with?"

"A hot redhead with a bod to die for. Maybe I should have asked her if she'd prefer a guy who isn't so ancient."

"It would probably take more than mere youth to entice a woman away from Wyatt McCauley," Cara said. "Now, let's get home. I've had a long day."

Her brother and sister quickly went on to other things, but Cara seethed the entire drive, delivering a silent sermon to herself about harnessing her feelings for Wyatt. Unfortunately, feelings weren't easily restrained. Probably the only protection was distance. That in mind, Cara resolved to issue a resounding "no" the next time Wyatt called for a date.

"No! What do you mean, no?" Wyatt had asked her out to dinner on Friday.

"No, as in I can't."

"Are you seeing someone else?"

"Is that any of your concern? Or is it your opinion I should reserve my time for you but leave you free to play the field?"

"What in blue blazes are you talking about?"

"Just what I said. You were in Oklahoma City, Monday, Dallas, Tuesday and back in Austin, Wednesday. Wednesday was a redhead...was Monday a blonde and Tuesday a brunette?"

"Glad you've been keeping up with my agenda."

"Actually I haven't," Cara countered, annoyed

with herself for letting her feelings surface. "But I ran into Frances at Barton Creek Mall and we took a shopping break together…had a nice little chat over coffee. She must have mentioned where you were. I like her, by the way."

"Wonderful. I'll tell her. OK, Frances reminded you of my travel schedule. But how did you know I was with a redhead on Wednesday?"

"Lucky guess," Cara said.

"Saw me, hmm? Well that redhead happens to be my sister."

"A red-haired sister? Spare me. You two couldn't look less alike."

"You'll have to take that up with my mother. She's the one who told us we were brother and sister. Do you want an affidavit from her?"

"Don't bother. I believe you…I guess."

"So what about dinner?"

Cara wavered. She'd been riddled with jealousy. Now she felt better, but still…no, better not to give in to temptation. Maybe it *was* his sister on Wednesday, but Wyatt hadn't denied going out with someone else on Monday or Tuesday. To him she was still just one of the masses. "I've already planned a picnic with Meg and Mark to watch the bats on Friday," she said truthfully.

"Picnic? Sounds good. I'm game."

"Just like that, you're coming along, huh?"

He chuckled. "Just like that. And since I'm crashing the party, I'll bring the food. Pick the three of you up at six.''

Cara gave no argument.

Wyatt arrived as scheduled, with a young boy in tow. "My nephew Danny," he said, introducing the carrot-top, freckle-faced child.

Cara smiled at the flaming hair. "I bet you look just like your mother."

"Except for the freckles," Wyatt noted.

"I like freckles," Cara said, patting Danny's shoulder as she called to Meg and Mark. The five of them walked out to the big Suburban Wyatt was driving tonight.

That date added another new dimension to Cara and Wyatt's relationship. Mark, who'd been unceasingly belligerent heretofore, began opening up to Wyatt, obviously warming to the man-talk. Also he developed a newfound respect of Wyatt's athleticism as the two older males entertained the young one with a rousing game of Frisbee.

"He's great, Sis," Meg said, leaning back on one of the blankets Wyatt had spread on the ground for them. They had selected a spot not far off the hike and bike trail near the Congress Avenue Bridge. "You *do* realize that Mark and I are old enough to know the score. If you and Wyatt want to…to…"

"To what?" Cara blushed in spite of herself.

"Oh, to have an affair. Get married. Start a family. Have a life together. Whatever. Follow your heart's desire, Cara."

Cara couldn't believe her ears. Not that such ideas hadn't occurred to her. In spite of her best efforts, Cara had thought about a future with Wyatt more than once, each time coming to the same conclusion—it'd never happen. "I'm just a diversion for him, Meg. It won't be long before he tires of the novelty and moves on to a fresh face."

"He sure puts on a good act for someone getting tired. How many men are willing to date a girl's whole family, and bring along part of his, too?"

Meg's words played on Cara's mind until the three guys returning from their game took her out of her reverie. Soon all settled in to a meal of fried chicken and potato salad.

"Is it time for the bats, Uncle Wyatt?" Danny's enthusiasm was endearing.

"Almost. Tell Cara, Meg and Mark about the bats." Wyatt sent a conspiratorial wink their way and leaned back on his arms to hear his nephew recite.

"There are about seven hundred and fifty *thousand* of them…" He looked to Wyatt for confirmation and at Wyatt's nod continued. "And they spend their summers underneath that bridge." Danny pointed to the structure. "At school I saw one of them up close. They're furry and about this big." He measured off a distance with his hands. "About the size of a big bird, only they're not birds, they're mammals…like us." He paused.

"Tell them what happens at dusk," Wyatt prompted.

"Oh, yeah. At dusk they leave their roost to spend the night hunting for insects to eat." As though his words had stirred the creatures, the first flurry of bats hit the air. "See, there they go!" The sky turned black with the spectacle of thousands of bats on the wing.

"Awesome," Mark said.

"Gross," Meg muttered. "Bats, yuck."

The dramatic show played out, Cara stood and began to gather their belongings. She swatted at her leg. "I wish one of your bats would zoom over and eat that mosquito," she told Danny.

"That would be neat," he said.

Meg disagreed as she dispatched a mosquito with a slap. "No bats for me, thank you. I'll deal with the mosquitoes on my own."

"Maybe there won't be any mosquitoes or bats at the yogurt shop," Wyatt said. "Anyone care to stop there for a cone? My treat."

"Double scoops?" Danny asked.

"Deal."

"With chocolate sprinkles on top?"

"Sure thing, pal. Anything else?"

"No."

"Then let's go."

After Danny had downed his frozen yogurt, he borrowed a pen from Wyatt and sketched a bat on a napkin, presenting it to Cara. He then drew one for Meg, who accepted it in spite of her anti-bat feelings, and another for Mark. On the drive back to the Breedons's house, he was still fixated on the animals. "Do you know what kind of bats we saw?'' He answered his own question. ''Mexican free-tails.''

''Someone's a regular encyclopedia,'' Cara said, smiling at the child.

''Uncle Wyatt teaches me.''

This was a completely new side of Wyatt McCauley, a side Cara liked very much. Perhaps he had cultivated the reputation of a Warren Beatty in his bachelor heyday, but tonight's outing had shown her a totally different man.

Danny was upstairs with Mark, viewing a rock collection amassed when Mark was about Danny's age. Meg was in the living room watching television, and Cara and Wyatt were sitting in the porch swing.

''It's been a nice evening,'' she said.

Wyatt turned her face to his. ''I can only think of one more thing that would make it ideal—this.'' He kissed her long and lovingly, his lips lingering on hers as if acknowledging the perfect match. Both of his hands now framed her cheeks, holding her in place. Not that she cared to free herself.

Both were breathing heavily when they ended the kiss. As Wyatt pressed her close in an embrace, Cara's line of vision took in the house over his shoulder. The window shade was pulled, but she could hear the sounds of Mark and Danny coming down to join Meg in front of the TV. ''We shouldn't be doing this here,'' she said.

''You mean, because of them?'' Wyatt chuckled. ''I doubt we're capable of competing with that comedian's monologue I hear. But you're right, anyway. I feel like I did when I was a teenager, holding my breath that Mom and Dad didn't switch on the light and expose my wandering hands.''

"So you had wandering hands, huh?''

"Still do.'' He caressed her neck with trailing fingertips, tracing the vee of her blouse down to the first button, which he began to undo.

She placed her hand atop his. "That's enough demonstration for a front porch.''

"Spend tomorrow with me, Cara. The whole day, just the two of us.''

"I have to work in the morning.''

"It's Saturday.''

"I have to work anyway.''

"Damn. The nuisance of loving a career woman. Maybe I should call that boss of yours and tell him not to work you so hard.''

Cara raised both hands. "Oh, no, you don't. It's better if you never even *meet* my new boss. Remember what happened with the last one.''

"OK, if that's the way you want it.'' He smiled. "At least you can joke about it now.''

"Only because getting fired turned out to be a blessing in disguise. I really lucked out.''

He kissed her hand. "You deserved the good fortune. Tell you what, if you'll see me tomorrow, I'll settle for the afternoon and evening. A movie and dinner?''

"I'd like that,'' Cara answered.

Later that night she lay in her bed, musing over Wyatt's "loving a career woman" statement. She knew the words had just slipped out. They didn't mean anything...did they?

As planned, Cara and Wyatt went to a Saturday movie, a three-hankie foreign film. "I didn't expect you to go for that kind of movie," she said, shading her eyes as they emerged from the darkness of the theater into the bright sunshine.

"It got good reviews. Two thumbs-up. But I'm not so testosterone ridden I can't appreciate all kinds of movies—including those aimed at the female persuasion. I'm a Walt Disney fan, too. Unfortunately, Danny's getting a little old for animations. I'm going to have to dig up another kid to watch Disney with."

Cara could easily picture that child. A pint-size version of Wyatt—dark hair, dark eyes and a smile to melt the female heart. "Oh, the theater would probably let you in. I don't think they bar unaccompanied grownups."

"Yeah, but it'd be bad for my macho image to go alone. Guess I'll just have to take you as my cover."

Wyatt suggested a home-cooked meal at his house and Cara readily concurred. She'd been curious as to where Wyatt lived and this was her opportunity to see. They stopped by Central Market for tuna steaks and salad fixings, then drove west toward Tarrytown.

Cara was surprised at what she found. Imagining Wyatt in a nineties brick-and-steel mansion straight out of *House Beautiful,* she couldn't believe the fifty-year-old bungalow that greeted her at the end of a sequestered drive. True, it sat on several acres of prime Austin land, but the structure itself was a low-slung house of modest proportions.

Wyatt opened his car door and came around to help with the groceries. "Don't make any rash judgments," he said. "What you are viewing is a work in progress. It may take me twenty years, but I intend to do most of the labor myself, so I'm renovating a little at a time. Come on in and see my handiwork and meet my housemates. Wyatt opened a door and they were greeted by two boisterous Irish setters, bodies swishing and tails wagging. "Jerry and Millie," Wyatt introduced the dogs.

"I recognize them from their picture in your office," Cara said. She petted the animals and looked around with unabashed approval at the welcoming home Wyatt had created for himself. White walls, unadorned windows, raised ceilings. Wyatt's place was understated, furnished simply and eclectically, yet inviting with its big brick fireplace, Ansel Adams photos and Oriental rugs.

They ate supper perched on pillows by the coffee table, the dogs lying off to the side, watchful in case a morsel of food accidentally fell.

"I wish it were winter," Cara said. "Then we could have a blaze in the fireplace."

"Even if we set the air conditioning at full blast,

it'd still be too darn hot today,'' Wyatt commiserated. "So you'll just have to take a rain check."

"OK, I'll jot it in my appointment book for December. One dinner in front of the fire."

"One *romantic* dinner in front of the fire," he corrected.

"It sounds as if you have more in mind than toasting marshmallows." Whatever Wyatt had in mind, the image was delightful. Cara closed her eyes and luxuriated in the thought. "I can see us now. Winter clothes...bulky sweaters and leggings."

"Leggings? No. I don't think they'll look that good on me."

"Me, doofus, not you. Even though you do have great legs."

"I didn't realized you'd noticed."

Believe me, I've noticed. "Anyway, back to my winter fantasy," Cara said. "We'll watch the snow falling outside the window and..."

Wyatt cupped her cheek with his palm. "Snowing? Austin hasn't had a good snow in years."

"Fantasy, remember? Now where was I...oh, yes, we warm ourselves with steaming hot apple cider and butter-coated popcorn."

"And then we make love in front of the hearth." He kissed her quickly. "I really like your fantasy."

"I'm beginning to wonder whether you have a one-track mind. I didn't say anything about making love."

"That doesn't mean it's not a great idea. In fact, we don't even have to wait until December." He placed a pillow nearer to the hearth and lay back on it, drawing Cara down against him. As his arms wrapped around her, pulling her close, she felt the firm contours of his masculine body. He began to kiss her, meaningful kisses.

Cara had already had a sample of Wyatt's kisses and they were wonderful. Denying herself now was close to impossible. But she couldn't let herself be trapped by her own hormones into McCauley's trophy corner. Wyatt had mentioned loving a career woman the night before, but Cara suspected he was more keen on making love than *being* in love. "I'm not sure I'm ready for this," she said, drawing back.

"It's your call." Wyatt might be irritated, frustrated, impatient, but his voice gave no hint of it. He sat up, then stood, reaching a hand down to Cara. "If we're not going to fantasize, might as well do something useful." They cleared away the dishes from the meal, coming back to sit on the couch, snifters of brandy in hand.

Wyatt watched her over his brandy glass. "Have you ever had a serious relationship, Cara? Ever been in love?"

The questions were unexpected. Although she and Wyatt were spending a substantial amount of time together, there had seemed to be an unspoken agreement about sharing too much.

"Once I thought I was. His name was Don, a fellow student at the university where I was studying. I met him about a year before Mom and Dad's accident, and developed an instant crush. He acted like he was crazy for me too, and we got engaged. I was so lovestruck I didn't notice that he was overbearing and controlling. Told me how to wear my hair, which classes to take, where we'd live after we married.

"But I didn't mind. I thought he was strong and decisive. Wrong. The minute I needed him, really needed him, Don wanted out. Said I was too clingy, too needy. Can you imagine? My parents had just died and I was too needy?"

"No, I can't imagine," Wyatt answered indignantly. "Too bad your champion of a brother was only a kid. He probably would have pummeled him."

Cara smiled. "How true. And at the time I would have cheered him on. I was devastated, thought I couldn't go on without someone in tandem to help carry the load. I had mistaken domination for support. But what do you know...not only did I manage, I even learned to like functioning solo. That spineless loser empowered me to be my own person. Unfortunately, you know what they say, once burned... I haven't dated much since." Staring off reflectively, Cara rested her case.

"Self-delusion is easy," Wyatt said. "And I oughta know, because I thought I was in love once, too. Looking back, I suspect it was more infatuation, lust, what have you. But I was so positive it was the real thing, I married her." He gave Cara a sideways glance. "Does that shock you?"

"Well...yes," she admitted. "I had you pegged as

a confirmed bachelor.'' Most people had tried marriage by the time they hit their mid-thirties, but the news that Wyatt had once committed his life to a woman he considered ''the one'' caught her off guard. ''When? For how long?''

''My second year in college. We eloped to Mexico on New Year's Eve. And 'how long'?'' He gave a sardonic laugh. ''The marriage didn't even make it to the end of the spring semester. Jocelyn, it turned out, had a problem with fidelity. She decided she wanted one of my fraternity brothers more than she wanted me. I decided to let her have him.''

Despite the nonchalant spinning of the tale, Cara could hear the hurt in Wyatt's tone and it took her by surprise. The man she once thought she knew would have walked away unscathed from a little thing like love on the rocks. In witnessing this revelation, Cara saw another layer peeled away from the devil-may-care image Wyatt had created for himself. Perhaps he'd flitted from woman to woman as a way of protecting his heart. She could understand that…she'd been cautious about protecting her own as well. ''I'm sorry,'' she told him.

She squeezed his hand.

''It happens.'' Wyatt shrugged unconcernedly. ''But enough talk of relationships gone awry. Too morbid.'' Wyatt hadn't planned on telling Cara about Jocelyn. As far as he was concerned, his past was private property. Bad enough that Frances was privy to so much of his early history.

Yet something about Cara caused him to say things he hadn't meant to say, to do things he didn't mean to do. Like making a commitment—even jokingly—for a date in December. What had possessed him? Uncomfortable with the thought, Wyatt purposely glanced at his watch. "It's getting late and I've got a golf game at seven a.m., so we'd better see about getting you home. Unless, of course, you'd like to sleep over?"

When Cara shook her head, he grinned. "Thought not. Pizza with Meg and Mark tomorrow night?"

Cara nodded.

"Hey, way to roll those dice, Wyatt, old man," Mark chortled. "You've landed on Park Place again. Welcome to Hotel Marky." He studied the card. "Let's see, you owe me—"

"I need to mortgage some property," Wyatt said to Meg who was serving as banker.

"Good thing you're better at real-life business than at Monopoly," Cara laughed.

"Ah, I'm just throwing the game to the three of you," Wyatt said.

"Sure you are." Mark jumped up from his chair at the ring of the doorbell. "Pizza's here."

Wyatt reached for his wallet and handed Mark a couple of bills. "The delivery guy will probably prefer this to Monopoly money."

"Good thing, because you don't have enough to pay for even one topping," Mark gibed.

Teasing aside, Cara saw respect in Mark's eyes. He and Wyatt had moved into an easy friendship. And Meg—Meg worshipped Wyatt. He wasn't really old enough to be her father, still he'd begun to fill a quasi-father role for Cara's younger sister. She sought his opinion on her studies, her boyfriends, even her designs—an area where Meg rarely allowed consultation, even from Cara.

"What are we doing next weekend, Wyatt?" her brother said as he placed the pizza boxes on a nearby table.

"Mark," Cara scolded. "Did it ever occur to you that Wyatt might have plans that don't include the Breedons?"

"Nope," Mark said jovially.

"Actually my plans for next weekend do include one of the Breedons."

"I'll bet that it's not anybody whose name starts with an 'M,'" Mark said as he crossed to the refrigerator and pulled out four soft drinks.

Once the meal was over, Meg and Mark excused themselves. A late movie beckoned.

Wyatt boxed the unfinished Monopoly game while Cara tidied the kitchen. She was putting the last plate into the dishwasher when he came up behind her, circling his arms around her waist. "Want to hear about my plans for the weekend?"

She wriggled out of his embrace and sat down at the table, inviting him to join her. "Something special?"

''It could be. I thought we'd run off to Padre Island Friday evening…'' He looked at Cara. ''How does that sound?''

Oh, how she wanted to go. Cara loved the seashore, walking along the beach in the moonlight, letting the waves caress her bare feet. But this would be a different weekend than the one in New Orleans. Things had changed between her and Wyatt. If she went with him, she would be saying ''yes'' to much more than a weekend trip. ''I have to work Saturday.''

''You've worked almost every Saturday since you started with Sweeney and Winslow. Surely you can get this one off. Afraid to be alone with me?''

''Of course not,'' she denied. ''We're alone right now.''

''So we are. And I plan to take advantage of it.'' Wyatt stood, then pulled her from her chair and into his arms. But he didn't ask for more from Cara than her kisses. Kisses she gave willingly.

CHAPTER EIGHT

EVEN though Cara hadn't gone along with Wyatt's plans for the beach, the two spent much of the weekend together anyway. On Saturday, they had dinner and rented a video and on Sunday finally made the visit to the Wildflower Center. Cara was grateful the press interest in them had waned, because Wyatt had begun to make a game of catch-as-catch-can kisses, even in public—capturing Cara behind a tree, at a stoplight. The kisses were brief and could hardly be called passionate; nevertheless, each one left her craving more.

Cara knew they couldn't keep on like this—hand holding, hugging, cuddling. Even if Wyatt continued being patient about not translating their feelings into stronger actions, Cara knew her own patience was growing thin. But she simply couldn't yield to those desires. The apprehension that Wyatt might fling her aside when the new wore off their relationship wouldn't go away.

When he brought her home around eight on Sunday evening, Meg and Mark were in the kitchen making chocolate chip cookies. "It was a great weekend," Wyatt said, stealing a glance in their direction before drawing Cara into his arms.

131

"They'll see us," she cautioned.

"So?" he whispered against her cheek. "They're a bit old to be discomfited by a few kisses."

"Not them, me. I'm the one uncomfortable about having witnesses." Cara pulled back, even though withdrawing from the sensual warmth of Wyatt's body tested every ounce of her fortitude. "You've already embarrassed me enough today," she said, shaking her head. "I was ready to hide beneath the dashboard when that guy in the car behind us on Burnet Road started pounding his horn."

"He was a spoilsport. Just because we didn't take off the instant the light turned green. You'd think he'd never passed the time with a little smooching."

"Is that the only reason you kissed me? To pass the time, stave off a bit of boredom?"

"Maybe not the *only* reason. But I must admit, kissing you is certainly not boring." He pulled her back into his arms.

"My goodness, you two are acting like lovebirds," Meg said laughingly. She was at the door between the kitchen and living room.

Still holding Cara, Wyatt tilted his head back. "Is that bad?" he asked Meg.

"Not as far as I'm concerned. Cara, the gang's going clubbing. We might be late. There are cookies on the cabinet—" she paused, "—in case you two need anything...sweeter. Ciao."

"Ciao," Wyatt echoed. The minute Meg was gone, he coaxed Cara's chin up with a knuckle so their lips could meet again. Nibbling the edge of her mouth, he whispered, "So is that what we are—lovebirds?"

Cara blushed but didn't answer. She'd worked so hard to keep her feelings for Wyatt in perspective, but the battle was proving too great. She'd told herself umpteen times that any moment he'd tire of her, move on to someone else. But it hadn't happened.

The Wyatt who caused her to be leery was not the one she'd come to know. This private Wyatt was good and kind and funny and considerate. He fit in with her family. The day had arrived for letting go of old fears. All that was keeping her from confessing her love was a need to know whether the feelings were reciprocal.

"You're saying a lot by not saying anything." Wyatt wanted to acknowledge her feelings, to reassure her, to say how important she'd become to him, how he wanted to spend the rest of his days with her. But he just couldn't get all the words out. They seemed to stick in his throat.

He *loved* her. Yet when all was said and done, had his aversion to marriage changed? Wyatt had seen the havoc wedding vows could engender. And not just his own experience. His sister Lily had endured a devastating divorce, too. Don't set yourself up for disaster was his mantra, as he'd scrupulously avoided commitment of any type. Even if he succeeded in overcoming his present fears, could he be sure that his love would stand the test of time? Wyatt wasn't sure he had that kind of faith in anyone—even himself.

"Meg." Cara's voice interrupted his agonizing.

"Meg what?"

"How did we let her maneuver us into this conversation?" She took a step backward, sitting down on the arm of the sofa.

"Human nature for her to assume. After all, we're not exactly behaving like enemies anymore. Besides, we've scheduled dates all the way to December." Wyatt's thoughts had drifted to that conversation, that fantasy scene, more than once. Even now, he could close his eyes and imagine them in front of his fireplace, doing a lot more than they'd done in real life.

Unable to resist, he touched Cara's cheek with his palm, bending to meet her lips. She was soft and giving, and his hands caressed her body, pulling her into his embrace. Cara didn't resist. Not until he started moving her toward the bedroom.

"I've got a busy day tomorrow," she said breathlessly, "and I know you do, too. You mentioned something about going in early so you could play hooky for an afternoon golf game."

"What if I decided to give up tomorrow's golf?"

"It wouldn't matter because I can't give up my job. Today has been wonderful, but I need to do some laundry and get to bed early."

"Getting to bed early is a great idea. I'll load the washing machine while you change into something more comfortable."

"Go home!" she ordered, laughing.

Reluctantly, Wyatt kissed her again and left. On the

drive to his house, he harked back to their conversation. Was Cara making sex hostage to a gold band? No, Wyatt knew her refusals weren't bargaining tools. She was simply being true to herself.

That was one of the things he admired most about Cara. He could trust her—she didn't play games. Still, he didn't know how much more of this such-good-friends arrangement he could take. There weren't enough cold showers on the North American continent to keep him at bay much longer.

On Monday afternoon, Wyatt watched as Wade Hendrix upended his putter into his golf bag, the score on the eighteenth hole and the game itself going to Wyatt.

"You son of a gun—you're as lucky in golf as you are with women," Wade said. "I guess drinks are on me again."

"Some guys have it. Others? What can I say?" Wyatt socked Wade's arm good-naturedly, then followed his friend, pulling their carts toward the clubhouse.

"Well, just to show you there are no hard feelings, Emily—that flight attendant I've been seeing—has an old college chum visiting from San Francisco. She's a physicist, lots of brains…beauty, too. Just your type. How about joining us for dinner tomorrow?"

"Thanks, but I'd better not."

"Why? Already have a hot date?"

Wyatt's started to answer "no," then caught himself. Wade knew Wyatt's view of marriage. He'd probably laugh himself silly if his buddy said that the only hot date he was interested in was busy Tuesday volunteering at the Rosemund Center. That he didn't care about meeting anyone new.

"Unless you've got another date or a multimillion dollar deal brewing, you've got to go. Emily says it's either doubles or me sitting home with a good book. So be a pal." Wade hesitated a second. "Don't forget I was willing to rush to your aid when you got into that firing mess after the auction."

"Yeah, but Cy was the one who came through."

"Only because he had a real vacancy and I would have had to invent one—which I would have done."

"All right, all right, you're the greatest."

"And to show you mean it, you'll double."

"Emily must be important."

"Very. So are you going to help out a buddy?"

Put that way, Wyatt found it difficult to refuse. Besides, he rationalized, maybe it was time to take a reality check, see how it felt being with another woman, before he continued pursuing happy-ever-afters with Cara.

The restaurant was four star and Ally Meadows, his dinner companion, was glamorous and charming. Even so, Wyatt had to restrain himself from glancing at his watch to see how much longer before he could make his excuses and duck out.

Ally's laugh seemed strident compared to Cara's. Her questions about his work came off more as polite conversation than actual interest. And taking her to bed? Unthinkable. The only woman he wanted there was Cara. It was long past time for him to accept the inevitable. Cara Breedon had hit him with a hammer blow to the heart.

Wyatt was debating how to handle that newfound knowledge when Frances confronted him the next morning. "You're seeing a lot of Cara Breedon," she observed as she delivered a carafe of freshly brewed coffee to Wyatt.

Wyatt waited for her to continue. He knew Frances was leading up to something.

"You know I adore you, Wyatt, but she's not the sort of woman—"

"Are you warning me to lay off, Frances?" Wyatt's lips curved in a grin. "Strange, since you were the one gung-ho about us having a true romance."

"So I'm having second thoughts," Frances said, sitting down in the chair beside his desk. "Especially after seeing today's newspaper." She handed Wyatt a section folded back to show a photograph of him with Ally Meadows.

He studied the photo. "Damn. I thought the media chase was over." Wyatt hadn't even spotted the picture being taken. Too late to close the barn door now, the damage was done. And if Frances was indignant over the picture, Cara had to be livid. "Damn," he repeated.

"My sentiments exactly. So what about Cara? She's a nice, sweet girl, Wyatt."

"And I'm Jack the Ripper?"

"You know what I mean. Cara's the kind of girl who falls in love, who expects marriage, children. I was hoping your thoughts might turn in that direction too, but…" Frances's voice trailed off as she shook her head disappointedly.

"How did you come to know so much about Cara?" Wyatt asked defensively. "A couple of short visits at the office and a coffee break at the mall give you so much insight?"

"Don't scoff," Frances scolded. "I can tell she's down to earth, sincere. And you…since Jocelyn, you've avoided involvements like the plague. Doesn't seem like you see Cara as permanent either. If you don't, then stop leading her on."

"I like being with Cara and she seems to enjoy my company too. What's wrong with that? She's a grown woman who can take care of herself. Besides, it isn't as if I've made any promises." He paused a second. "I know better than that."

Frances winced and Wyatt suppressed a grin. He couldn't help needling Frances. She was like a mother who'd picked out the ideal wife candidate for her son, only to have him foul things up.

Wyatt wasn't making any explanations to Frances just yet. Cara had a right to know his feelings before he shared them with anyone else.

"Cara Breedon is a woman who expects a man's pledge. At least, she will eventually. Just be careful you don't break her heart." Frances stood up. "And that's the end of my advice for today."

"Can I count on that?"

Frances answered him with a cutting glance before returning her attention to business. "Why don't I place that call to Singapore now? If we don't hurry, your prospective client will be in bed."

Wyatt talked with the client and arranged a conference call for next week. Once the conversation terminated, he sat at his desk, mulling over Frances's admonitions. She'd asked if he saw Cara as permanent. Yes, definitely permanent.

Cara was a woman any man could fall in love with and he'd tumbled like a barrel over Niagara Falls. *Love*...when...how it'd happened, Wyatt didn't know. It seemed some overwhelming force had taken over his mind and body, governed his actions since the day he'd met her. What other excuse was there for the way he'd pursued her, for making that insane bid at the auction? Love was as good an explanation as any.

All he knew was that, despite Cara's insinuations that he was a human dating machine, and Frances all but telling him to curb his tom-catting ways, the fact was Ally was the only woman other than Cara that he'd dated since the auction. And if it weren't for Monday's golf game with Wade, that wouldn't have happened. He'd have sat at home last night. Sat at home thinking about Cara.

Frances stuck her head back in the door. "Since

you're finished with Singapore, do you want that meeting with the finance staff? You mentioned seeing them today.''

Wyatt motioned for her to come in. ''Maybe later this afternoon,'' he said, then added like a fisherman casting out bait, ''I think I'll call Cara instead, see if she's free for lunch.''

Frances's expression demanded an explanation.

''You're absolutely right about her,'' Wyatt conceded. ''She's not only the type of woman who expects promises, she deserves them.'' And Wyatt intended to make plenty—promises in a church, he and Cara standing before a minister. But Frances could wait to hear all those details. He had to see Cara first.

''Last night meant nothing,'' he assured Frances. ''Cara was busy, Wade said his date had a friend in town and asked me to go along as a favor. The friend was nice, but the evening was torture—simply because she wasn't Cara.

''You'll be relieved to know that as far as I'm concerned, my relationship with the lady is an exclusive one. Maybe I needed last night to prove that to myself. But rest easy, I adore Cara. I love her company, have grown intensely fond of her brother and sister, respect her rock-solid lifestyle. Heaven help me, I've even begun to hope the dogs can get along with her cat, that Jerry and Millie won't chase poor Flake around the house.''

Frances's smile showed he was back in her good graces.

And this was no con job on Wyatt's part. Every word he'd uttered was true. He *did* adore Cara. He reveled in small insignificant things when he was with her, wanted to share commonplace details of his life with her. At least a dozen times a day he was tempted to phone her, just to hear her voice. And the thought of making love to her caused him to...his body began to stir. *The office isn't the place to think about love-making with Cara,* he cautioned himself, grateful for the buzz of the intercom, which jarred him back to the present.

"You have a visitor, Mr. McCauley," the receptionist told him. "Says she's an old friend."

"Does this friend have a name?"

"She said she wanted to surprise you. I told her you don't see people without an appointment, but she's insisting."

"Hello, Wyatt." A new voice was on the line. *Jocelyn.* He hadn't heard her speak in over a dozen years, but the breathy, whispery tone was unchanged.

"Come down to the lobby and rescue me from your guard dog."

Wyatt rang off, shaking his head. "You won't believe who's downstairs," he told Frances. "Jocelyn. Waiting to see me."

"As I live and breathe." Frances placed a hand across her chest. "I thought you were rid of that scheming female forever. What does she want?"

"Nothing good, I'm sure."

"Just like a bad penny, she shows up again,"

Frances said. "Do you want me to go down and run her off?"

"Nah, I might as well see her. Then send her on her way. Would you go fetch her?"

"I'd rather boot her out the door with a kick to the behind."

"You may still get your chance. But in the meantime, we'd better find out what she's up to."

Minutes later a statuesque brunette stood framed in his doorway. "Hello, Wyatt," she said. "Surprised?"

He studied her, taking in the tanned, athletic figure displayed to good advantage in the short tight dress. "Yes, I must admit I am. Hello, Jocelyn."

"Well, may I come in?"

"Oh, sure." He motioned her to a chair in front of his desk.

Jocelyn sat and crossed her long legs, the skirt riding up to mid-thigh. She placed her straw purse on the floor, then pushed back in her chair, folding her hands in her lap. Clearly she knew Wyatt was taking in every move.

Wyatt watched carefully. The years had been kind to her. She looked wonderful, more beautiful now than as a coed, beautiful enough to make a man forget she couldn't be trusted out of his sight. A man with a short memory. As far as Jocelyn was concerned, Wyatt's memory was as dependable as the most sophisticated computer.

"I suppose you're wondering why I'm here," she said.

"Well, we haven't exactly been in close contact lately."

"Unfortunately." She gave him a warm smile, showing white-white teeth. "That's because I was married again and living in California."

"Again? What is this, three, four?"

"Don't be mean. Anyway, it hardly matters since I'm single now and back in Austin. I had to see you."

"Oh?"

Jocelyn fiddled with her necklace and seemed to be searching for a way to present her message. "This is rather awkward...but I wanted to let you know that I've never forgotten how it was with us."

"Oh?" he repeated. "As I recall, I was pretty forgettable when you took up with Blake, made him husband number two."

"Really, Wyatt. You're not going to hold past sins against me, are you? After all, I was a young, immature girl. Now I'm a grown woman."

"That you are," he said appreciatively. His ex-wife had blossomed spectacularly. Still, the bloom was off the rose in Wyatt's eyes.

Jocelyn had apparently seen the brief spark of approval, because she reached across the desk and touched his hand. "How about lunch for old times' sake?"

"Old times? We must have had all of thirteen months together. If you count from the first meeting to our parting, that is. Not much to base a reunion on."

"Come on Wyatt, don't be so stuffy. Be a good boy and take Jocelyn to lunch."

Wyatt sat quietly, giving her another appraising stare. Back in college, this coquettish routine would have had him jumping through hoops. No longer. Besides, there was Cara. He had better plans for lunch than reminiscing with his ex-wife. "Sorry, Jocelyn. I'm not available—for lunch or anything else."

"Well, I had hoped to keep this cordial," she said, her voice huffy. "However, if you don't have time for a social meal, then perhaps you can eke out a couple of hours for a business one."

"I wasn't aware we had anything to talk about on that score."

"Au contraire, Wyatt dear. This little operation you started in our tiny apartment has certainly grown." She gestured to indicate the impressive surroundings.

"Get real, Jocelyn. There was no business then, just one lowly computer."

"My lawyer thinks otherwise."

"Are you trying to say you're here to claim a share?"

"Surely I'm entitled." She stood. "Let's talk about it in a more pleasant setting."

From the moment she opened the morning newspaper and saw that picture of Wyatt, Cara had been on pins and needles, waiting to hear from him, hoping for a story that was different from what she feared.

Since Sunday, she'd ceased worrying about Wyatt's motives, telling herself that even if his initial interest in her had begun as a diversion, the interest had lasted long enough to smack of something deeper. Then that dratted picture had appeared and shaken her confidence. Now it had been a whole four hours since she'd laid eyes on it—but no contact from Wyatt. Still Cara was willing to give him the benefit of the doubt. Maybe he hadn't seen the paper yet.

If the invitation for lunch had come from anyone but Cy Winslow, she would have declined and continued monitoring the telephone. But Cy had asked, telling her it was company policy for one of the partners to get to know a new employee better. And Cara knew she had no choice but to accept.

So now she was dining at Green Pastures with Cy, pretending to be a normal person and not the nervous wreck that lurked beneath the surface.

"How are things going with the firm?" he asked, taking a sip of his iced tea. "Are you glad you joined us?"

"Oh, yes. I love my job," Cara said sincerely. "Everyone's been so supportive. And the staff are really top-notch."

"Good. The feeling is mutual. I get glowing reports about your performance all the time. What else do you like besides work? Sports, antiques, music?"

"Sports, spectator only. Antiques, so-so," she wiggled her hand. "Music, definitely yes."

"Then maybe we can see a musical together. A

road show revival of *Chorus Line* is in town and I've got a couple of Thursday night tickets. Would you care to go?''

Cara studied Cy Winslow. He had been cordial in the office, but completely professional, no hint of a personal interest. Now, however, this meal had taken an unexpected turn. Cara knew she should be flattered. Women at the office literally sighed whenever Winslow walked by, and as far as she knew, she was one of the few he'd asked for a real date.

''I'd never have invited you out if I hadn't seen that shot of McCauley and friend in this morning's newspaper. After the auction and all the resulting publicity, I'd assumed you two were an item. Guess I was wrong.''

Cara wondered if the pain in her soul showed on her face when Cy took her hand. ''Wyatt's a great guy, but he has a short attention span when it comes to women. I have to say though, you've held his interest longer than any other woman I can remember.''

And that's supposed to make me feel better? ''We've gone out a few times,'' Cara hedged, wishing they could talk about something else and hoping against hope that Cy didn't ask for details about the auction. Or worse, want to know what investment guru had generated enough pocket money for her to make that outlandish bid. It had been mentioned again in the brief article about Wyatt and his new cutie, bringing up old embarrassments along with that stab of alarm that she might indeed be slated for relegation to the shelf.

Fortunately, Cy was more tactful than to mention the auction; instead he shifted the conversation back to Thursday. "So, are you up for *Chorus Line*?"

Cy was debonair, handsome as all get-out, and genuinely nice to boot, but Cara didn't want to lead him on. With or without Wyatt, her priorities were the same...almost. Meg and Mark and her career, that's what mattered.

It was at that very moment she gazed across the restaurant and spied him—Wyatt. And with a woman. A different one, no less. The Tuesday night companion looked to be petite and blonde. This was a striking brunette with a deep tan. Cara's heart recoiled in anguish. All morning she'd tried to convince herself that picture meant nothing. After all, no one knew better than she how the press could distort a situation.

But here he was in person—the two-timing rat. She could see things for herself, could see all too clearly. Just when she'd begun believing there could be a future with Wyatt, suddenly he'd reverted to past ways.

"It usually doesn't take a woman that long to make up her mind to go out with me," Cy kidded.

Cara forced her awareness back to Cy. "I bet it doesn't. Thank you for the invitation." She glanced back toward Wyatt. A red-tipped fingernail was stroking the hand he'd rested on the white linen tablecloth.

"I'd love going to *Chorus Line* with you," she heard herself answer.

Wyatt had suppressed a surge of jealousy when he'd walked into the restaurant and noticed Cara there, sitting with Cy Winslow. A surge that resurfaced every time he stole a glance their way. But he couldn't concentrate on Cara at the moment. He was too busy fending off Jocelyn and her threats to relieve him of a chunk of his income. He had to assume a tough stance with Jocelyn, even if his attention was split between her and his own burning desire to march across the room and plant a fist on Winslow's chiseled chin.

"My lawyer warned me years ago you might launch a strike someday—" he paused a moment "—and he *also* said your case was as weak as watered-down whiskey."

"Then you got some poor legal advice."

Wyatt chuckled derisively. "Do you honestly think this lawyer you've hired can pull off an absurd demand for fifty percent of my company? I don't recommend you risk it in court. But I'll tell you what I'm prepared to offer and if you're smart, you'll go along because this will be my only offer. If you don't accept, then we'll have that court battle." Wyatt took a pen and business card from his pocket, jotted a figure on the back of the card, then handed it to Jocelyn.

She read the amount and shot him an angry frown.

"Well?" he asked.

"How soon can you get the damn money?"

"Finish your coffee and we'll go back to the office to draw up an agreement," he said. Once you've ceded all past and future interests in my company, you can leave with the 'damn money.'" Wyatt hated giving her a dime, but he knew buying her off would save him both time and money, as well as future aggravation.

He should have been feeling triumphant and he might have, if it weren't for that cozy tête-á-tête on view a dozen tables away. Some friend Cy was. Cara belonged to *him*. And the minute he freed himself from Jocelyn's tentacles, Wyatt intended to make sure that Cara and Cy—plus everyone else in Austin—understood that.

CHAPTER NINE

"Too bad you've got that training session scheduled this afternoon, it's a beautiful day to waste on work," Cy said as they were driving back to the Sweeney and Winslow building.

"Isn't it," Cara answered, in truth grateful for that training session. From the second she'd agreed to the date with Cy, Cara had regretted the impulsive action. She was holding her breath hoping that he didn't suggest they forget work and delight in the sunshine together. "But as a new employee, I can't risk being a truant." Cara gave a nervous laugh.

"I wish everyone we hired was as conscientious." Cy pulled into his personal parking space and circled the car to open the door for Cara. "I enjoyed lunch. Six-thirty Thursday for *Chorus Line*? We can grab a quick bite before the play."

"Six-thirty's fine," Cara said, wondering what she'd gotten herself into. And suspecting she knew all too well. Being upset with Wyatt was no reason to go courting trouble—and dating one's boss was exactly that. But a bit late for regrets now. She couldn't very well tell Cy she'd changed her mind thirty minutes after accepting his invitation.

"Great," he said. "Now I'm exercising a boss's

prerogative and taking the afternoon off. Don't work too hard in my absence. That's a direct order," he said jokingly, then climbed back into his Porsche and gave a jaunty salute of farewell.

Relieved, Cara waved back. Cy Winslow might be one of the firm's partners, and he might have asked her out, but it didn't appear he intended to push too hard. At least she hoped that was the case.

The training session took the entire afternoon and since Cara's role was simply to sit back and listen, she had an abundance of time to ponder the events at lunch. And while that lunch had been shared with one incredibly handsome man, most of her thoughts were on another.

Perhaps she'd misconstrued what she saw at the restaurant. For all she knew, Wyatt's lunch companion was a client and the meeting completely innocent. But Cara couldn't erase from her mind the woman's flirtatious manner, or the fact that the night before there had been a different woman with him. Definitely a message there—a message confirming that Cara Breedon wasn't as important to Wyatt McCauley as she'd fancied herself to be.

"Your calls, Ms. Breedon." The receptionist handed her several pink slips as she emerged from the training session.

Cara reached her office, returned the lone business call of the bunch, then sat there staring at the other notes. All were from Wyatt. The last said, "I'll be in the office until six. Call me when your meeting ends."

She picked up the receiver, then put it down.

Cara wasn't ready to talk to Wyatt just yet. All her fretting had caused a headache to form in her left temple. She'd go home, call him from there. Or not. Just because he'd beckoned didn't mean she had to respond like a trained seal. It was high time Wyatt understood that.

Meg was home when she walked in. Cara pitched her purse onto the kitchen table, set her briefcase on a chair, and informed her sister, "My head's killing me and I'm off to bed. Unless the house catches on fire, don't disturb me."

"A headache?" Having heard no word from Cara, Wyatt had driven over, a bouquet of mixed blossoms in his hand and as many mea culpas at the ready as necessary. He suspected Cara was angry. Now he didn't know what to think. Her being ill worried him. That is, if she really was.

"That's what Cara told Meg," Mark said, inviting him in. "And she hasn't made a peep since I've been home. Want to hang around in case she surfaces? I was just fixing sandwiches."

Wyatt followed Mark to the kitchen and watched him assemble three huge ham and cheese sandwiches. "Want one?" Mark offered.

"No thanks." With his stomach twisted in a knot, nothing was appetizing. Nor was waiting around to see Cara. Wyatt had spent the entire afternoon anticipating her call and he was tired of it. Could she really have a headache, or simply be indulging herself in a fit of pique? It wasn't like her to sulk, but then he'd hardly been himself since he'd witnessed that cozy scene betwen Cara and Cy at the restaurant, either. His machinations at work had been prime entertainment for Frances this afternoon.

"Never thought I'd see Wyatt McCauley suffering a bout of the green-eyed monster," she'd observed.

"Don't be ridiculous. I'm not jealous."

"Of course not. But would you be pacing a hole in your carpet if you'd caught Cara with Ralph Sweeney?"

"Ralph? What's he got to do with anything?"

"A Sweeney and Winslow policy is that one of the partners takes each new employee to lunch. Did it ever occur to you that Cy was simply carrying out company protocol?"

It hadn't. Wyatt had forgotten the much-touted policy, surprising, in view of the number of times Cy had suggested he do the same, how it enhanced employee morale. Well, too bad the partner escorting Cara *wasn't* Ralph Sweeney. Ralph was not only a good seventy-five pounds overweight and pushing fifty, but he was also happily married with three kids.

Wyatt sighed knowingly. He couldn't blame Cy for ensuring that he got the honors with this particular employee. Cara's delicate beauty would be tough for any red-blooded boss to ignore. But he vowed to make his friend understand that Cara would not be available for repeat performances.

"Wyatt?" Mark was snapping his fingers in front of Wyatt's nose. "Where'd you go?"

"What? Oh, yeah, just thinking about the office. Guess I'll take that sandwich, after all. Got any beer?" Wyatt stayed at the Breedon house until almost ten, but no Cara. Once or twice he was tempted to burst into her bedroom and ask if he could bring an aspirin, cold compresses...an engagement ring. But if she was sleeping he didn't want to awaken her.

Cara spent the night brooding and nursing her headache. By morning, the headache was gone and decisions were made. As soon as she got to work, she'd call Wyatt. She knew he had come by last night. She'd heard him talking, and this morning Meg had taken obvious pleasure in showing her the flowers he'd brought. Cara had no doubt he would phone again at first opportunity. She intended to beat him to the punch. Forget waiting to call. Since Wyatt was always in the office early, she'd stop by before she went to work.

As Cara rode up on the elevator, she tried to formulate a speech. The words wouldn't fall into place. Better maybe to hear Wyatt out before she said anything. Cara had accepted the fact that she had no idea what was going on with Wyatt and those two females he'd been with. So she'd listen first, then make her judgments accordingly. The one thing she was absolutely certain about was that Wyatt McCauley wasn't going to continue to dominate her life. Except for work, she'd become deferential to him, letting all her energies center around him, a planet orbiting his sun. Not good. And all too reminiscent of a younger Cara. A Cara she'd sworn never to be again.

"Wyatt?" she called as she tapped on his door, then pushed it open. Frances wasn't in yet.

"Well, good morning," he drawled, quickly punching a button on his computer as he stood. "I hope your headache's better."

"It is."

"This is a nice surprise, the perfect way to start a day." He came around the desk and kissed her on the cheek. "I was waiting until nine before dialing you. Afraid of waking you if you were still sick. We need to talk."

"Yes." Cara moved away from him. She couldn't let Wyatt's kisses affect her thinking.

"I guess you saw me yesterday." He reached for his coffee carafe and poured each of them a cup.

"At lunch or in the morning paper?" Cara took the coffee and settled silently into a chair. Let him twist in the wind. She had no intention of making this easy for him.

Wyatt rubbed a hand across his jaw. "Am I in trouble?"

"Why should you be in trouble? We have no 'understanding.' You're free to go out with anyone you choose."

"In case you hadn't noticed, I've been choosing you."

"I'm a big girl, mature enough to concede that our dates didn't necessarily mean anything."

"Maybe not to you. They meant a hell of a lot to me." Wyatt put a rein on his temper, then eyed her closely. "So you came to my office first thing in the morning merely to announce you don't give a hoot who I date?"

"No," Cara admitted. "I came to…to… I know you don't have to give me explanations, but I suppose I came here to ask for them anyway."

Wyatt knelt beside her chair and took her hand in his. "I got roped into taking Ally Meadows to dinner—a favor for a pal. I planned to tell you all about it, then that photographer beat me to the draw. But I promise—" he made an X across his heart "—I spent the entire evening wishing I was with you."

"You did?" Cara felt herself weakening.

"Yes. Nothing against Ms. Meadows, but that night was our first and last date. I only want to be with one woman from now on." He raised her hand to his lips and kissed the fingertips. "Forgive me?"

Wyatt seemed so sincere, those dark eyes so warm and bidding. But she'd heard only half of the story. "And the lunch date? Surely she wasn't a favor, too?"

Wyatt groaned. "Not hardly. The second woman was Jocelyn."

"Your ex-wife?" Cara blurted in astonishment. Somehow she'd hoped Jocelyn had aged poorly, with leathery skin and multiple chins. No such luck. Jocelyn was drop-dead gorgeous.

"She came for her piece of the corporate pie. Now that I'm older and successful, suddenly I'm much more appealing to her—me and my money, anyway."

"And?"

"And nothing. She doesn't appeal to me one whit. In fact, I actually paid her off to make her go away. Like I've been trying to tell you, I only find *one* woman appealing." He rose, gazing down at her. "Have breakfast with me and I'll fill in all the details."

"I can't. Work, you know." She glanced at her watch and stood. "I need to leave in a few minutes."

Wyatt stroked her cheek. "Lunch, then?"

"I'm driving down to San Marcos at noon to meet a client."

"No problem. We'll make it dinner. See you at seven."

Cara sighed. "I can't have dinner with you, either." She still wasn't completely mollified about Wyatt's escapades of the past two days, but she wasn't about to turn loose of him. "Would tomorrow be all right?"

"Of course." Wyatt slapped his forehead. "Where's my brain? I should have realized you're not up to going out tonight. What you need to do is go home instead of to the office. You may be new on the job but no one expects you to come in sick, client or no client. Go home and baby yourself. Then, if you're not better, I'm insisting you see a doctor.''

''I'm fine. Honest. It was just a headache, nothing more. The reason I can't have dinner with you is because I've already made plans for this evening.''

''The Rosemund Center again?''

Wyatt's presumption aggravated Cara. Did he think he could flaunt women all over town while the best she could do with her spare time was volunteer at the Rosemund Center? ''No, I've made a date.''

Silence. ''I see. Then I suppose I'm fortunate you can pencil me in tomorrow.'' More silence.

Oh, what's the use. I'm no good at pretense. ''I'd rather be with you,'' she said softly.

''Oh, you would?'' Wyatt visibly relaxed and his voice lowered seductively. ''So why don't you break the date?''

''Can't. I did a dumb thing. Agreed to go out with my boss.''

Wyatt was clearly taken aback. ''I was jealous as heck when I caught sight of you with Cy. Then I dismissed it as a business lunch. I should have known better. He's quite a ladies' man.''

''It started out as a business lunch and then we spotted you—''

''So you were jealous too?''

''As you put it, jealous as heck. I could have cheerfully punched Jocelyn's lights out. For a nonviolent person, I entertain gruesome thoughts when it comes to you and other females.''

Wyatt laughed. "I know exactly what you mean. I feel like ringing up Cy and threatening to work him over if he takes out my girl."

"*Your* girl?"

"My girl. My *only* girl."

"Now that's good to know. But you'd better let me handle this situation myself. After all, he is your friend as well as my boss."

"OK. As long as you spend the hours between now and tomorrow evening—even those hours with Cy—thinking of me."

As if I could think of anything else. She blew him a kiss and left.

"I don't usually mix business and pleasure," Cy said. He'd stopped by Cara's office to ask if he could pick her up at six instead of six-thirty so they could have a more leisurely dinner. "And I'm getting the impression that I may have crossed a line in asking you out. That you may be having second thoughts."

Cara didn't realize she'd been so transparent. "Am I that obvious?" she asked, "or are you just remarkably perceptive?"

"Remarkably perceptive, naturally." Cy leaned forward in his chair and rested his forearms on her desk. "If you want to cancel, there'll be no hard feelings. I shouldn't have put you on the spot."

"That's not it. Frankly, there's another reason...Wyatt. He, that is, we—"

"Say no more," Cy broke in. "Wyatt's as important a friend as you are an employee. What do you say we skip going to the play, forget this little episode ever happened and get back to business?''

''I'd like that.''

''Great. By the way, I hear you've picked up two new accounts for us...one just today.''

''It took several hours in San Marcos, but yes, we do have a new client.''

''Good going. Jeff Mayo told me I was crazy when I instructed him to hire you. Said Brooke would make our lives miserable if we did. But Brooke's shown herself as all bark, no bite, and Jeff's become one of your biggest supporters. Of course, Wyatt's word has always been good as gold. When he recommends—''

''Wyatt?'' Cara croaked, interrupting the rest of his sentence. She could feel the color draining from her face.

Cy slapped his forehead. ''Gosh, have I messed up again? I thought you probably knew by now that he'd asked his compadres to help him out.''

''His compadres?''

''Yeah, he hit on me, Wade Hendrix, and Glenn Gaston over drinks. The three of us got quite a charge out of a woman having McCauley in a dither. Never thought we'd see the day he'd cast himself in the role of knight in shining armor. Of course, after I met you, I could understand all too well.''

Cara shook her head. Wyatt's shining armor was developing a distinct tarnish. ''I didn't realize he tried to foist me off on everyone in the business. I was swell-headed enough to believe I got this job on merit.'' Her shoulders sagged as the facts of the situation sank in.

''It's not as bad as that. We were all quite willing to take you on. And regardless of how you got it, you've earned your place by now,'' Cy tried to assure her. ''Wyatt really did me a favor, not the reverse.''

''Now you're flattering me.''

''Not in the least. What about those new clients? That's significant.''

As if sensing her distress, Cy kept on singing her praises, but Cara had difficulty concentrating on a single word he said. All she could think about was how Wyatt had taken over—again.

''Cara, I'm sorry I upset you by mentioning Wyatt's involvement.''

''Don't worry about it, Cy. If I'd thought it through, I'd have realized he was behind it.'' *He does get a charge out of interfering in my life.*

''Well, all right. Just don't judge him too harshly. He meant well.''

''You men...always stick together,'' she said, forcing a hint of humor in her tone. Cy had done nothing wrong. Wyatt was the culprit here. She'd not take out her hostilities on someone else.

''You OK, then?''

''Fine.'' She gave a thumbs up.

''Well, I'd better let you get back to work,'' he said.

''Yeah. These Sweeney and Winslow guys are really brutish if you don't keep your nose to the grindstone.'' She smiled to show she was teasing.

Cy left her office with one of his trademark jaunty salutes.

The instant he was gone, Cara picked up her telephone and dialed Wyatt. ''I'll arrive home at five-thirty. Be there!''

''You broke your date for me?'' Wyatt's voice held undisguised pleasure.

''Yes, and now I'm ready to break your nose.'' Cara hung up the receiver.

When she parked in her driveway several hours later, Wyatt was already there, sitting in the porch swing. He rose to meet her, pulling her toward him for a kiss.

''I don't want your kisses,'' she said, shoving him away. ''I want explanations.''

''More? All right. I'll tell you anything you want to know. Where do you want to start? Ally? There's really not much more to tell. Jocelyn?'' He tugged Cara toward the porch swing and sat down, setting the swing in motion. ''Or would it be my getting you the job at Sweeney and Winslow?''

''I should have known Cy would warn you about spilling the beans. I thought I could trust you, but you're conniving, sneaky, underhanded—''

''Now that we've covered my good points, do you want to tell me why you're so danged teed-off that I helped?''

''Helped? By calling a powwow, discussing my situation with complete strangers—at least to me—then leaning on them to give me a job.''

"And that's so terrible?"

"If you recall, I specifically told you not to interfere.''

"I caused the problem, so I fixed it. Where's the big sin?"

"You could have told me what you'd done.''

"Yeah? You were being so stubborn, you wouldn't have accepted the offer if you'd known I had anything to do with it. Just look how you're reacting now.''

"That may be true, but can't you understand the principles at stake here? You've had a dozen opportunities to tell me since then. One of those occasions where I was embarrassing myself, rambling on about my good fortune should have opened the door to a confession.''

"Maybe. But you were so happy and I—''

"Didn't want to burst my bubble?"

"Exactly. I like seeing you happy, Cara. I love you.''

"You don't know the first thing about love. Love to you is taking over, managing every situation. And you've managed me from day one, ever since you compromised the auction. What did you think? That after buying me for the weekend, you had a right to do whatever you wished with my life?"

"I didn't buy you.''

"Of course not. You merely donated a hundred thousand to the Rosemund Center out of the goodness of your heart.'' She jabbed her index finger at his chest. "I take that back. You don't have a heart.''

"Now wait a damn minute.'' Wyatt's temper was rising. Maybe Cara had a right to be a little peeved, but everything he'd done, he'd done for her. Couldn't she see that? "You're being just plain irrational,'' he said.

"Am I? Is it irrational to want to run one's own life? You've been exercising entirely too much influence over mine. And I won't allow it to continue.'' She stood, arms crossed defensively, and stared down at him. "You're probably the type of man who thinks the ideal woman is placid and subservient.''

"Well, my ideal woman's damned sure not a screaming shrew.''

"I have a right to scream.''

"Then yell away. Let the whole neighborhood know what a louse I am.''

Cara opened her mouth to protest, then thought better of it. A shouting match in the front yard wasn't at all seemly. "I don't like being controlled,'' she said between clenched teeth.

Wyatt got up and came over to her, backing her up against the porch post. "So you think I've been controlling?''

"I don't think...I know.''

"And what about this? Is this part of my controlling, too?'' His parted lips met her closed ones.

Cara tightened her lips even more. *He can kiss me till hell freezes over...I will not respond.* He could caress her all he wanted, trace her spine with his fingers like he was doing now till he wore the tips off, but she'd never... Her heart began racing as Wyatt nuzzled her ear, then rained kisses on the plane of her cheek. When his lips began moving down her neck toward the edge of her neckline, her heart pounded in her chest like a tom-tom and she could hear her own rapid breathing.

By the time he turned her loose, Cara's body burned as hot as a mass of glowing red embers. Her determination to resist him had vaporized in the heat.

Cara knew she should slap his face, tell him off, do something in protest. But after that kiss—well, it was all she could do to stay on her feet. She just stared mutely as he disappeared into the night.

Cara returned to the porch swing with conflicting emotions—not knowing whether to be angry or disappointed...with herself or Wyatt or both. She knew she'd carried on like a harpy, but she had a right to. What Wyatt had done was wrong.

For years she'd been hoping for a job like the one she had now. Couldn't Wyatt understand that the mere knowledge she hadn't achieved it on her own took away the joy, not to mention what it did to her confidence? Just thinking about going into the office tomorrow, knowing she was there on sufferance, made her angry all over again. She sat there stewing another fifteen minutes before going inside.

Meg was sitting at the kitchen table drinking a glass of skim milk when Cara finally went in, slamming the door behind her. Mark was rummaging in the refrigerator.

"I didn't know you two were here," she said.

"Like you'd notice with all that fussing and shouting." Mark carried a container of leftover spaghetti to the cabinet. "Anyone else hungry?"

"No, Mr. Human Garbage Disposal," Meg jabbed, pushing her glass aside. "Cara, we heard Wyatt's voice, then him driving away. What's going on?"

"Yeah, why the raised voices?" Mark put a plate of spaghetti in the microwave to heat. With one hand resting on the top of the humming microwave, Mark stared at his sister. "Well, don't keep us in suspense. What's the problem? What'd Wyatt do?"

"Play God, as usual. Just when I decided to put the auction mess behind me, I learn he's responsible for my new job. I was hired by Sweeney and Winslow only because Wyatt pressed Cy Winslow into helping out."

"What's so bad about that? You think the job's terrific. You ought to be grateful to Wyatt." Mark opened the microwave and rotated his plate.

"Grateful? Just like a *male* to take that point of view."

"Just like a *female* to think a good turn's some sign of a personality disorder." Although Mark made a habit of squabbling with Meg, he seldom talked back to Cara.

"Now wait a sec," Meg intervened, playing peacemaker for a change. "This isn't a male or female thing. But I'll have to say, Cara, you do seem a trifle overwrought." She patted her sister's shoulder consolingly.

"A trifle overwrought?" Cara stood up and started pacing the kitchen. "I'm not a trifle overwrought—I'm plain mad! I asked Wyatt to let me handle things myself. So what does he do? Ignores me and handles it anyway—in secret."

"Give the guy a break," Mark said, sitting down. "You need to stop ranting and raving. He did something for your own good."

Cara glared at Mark. "Your loyalties have certainly shifted. I don't want Wyatt or anyone else for that matter, doing something *for me* if it's against my wishes."

"That's just because you're so used to running everything." Meg was walking alongside Cara, massaging her shoulders. "I'm with Mark and Wyatt on this one. From the time Mom and Dad died you've been in charge, in total control. Relinquishing a bit of power to someone else won't exactly tip the world off its axis, now will it?"

"Psychology this semester?" Cara grumbled. She needed sympathy here, not her two siblings backing Wyatt's cause. Maybe the earth was in no danger of tipping, but *her* world had definitely turned upside down.

"Try to see it from his perspective," Meg went on soothingly. "He only wanted to take care of you. What's so evil about that? It's been a long time since you had anyone take care of you.''

Cara dropped back into her chair, putting her head on her arms. She was too tired to argue anymore and it was clear Meg and Mark weren't about to see her point, even if she argued all night. They just didn't get it. Not any more than Wyatt had.

''Sleep on it and you'll see we're right,'' Mark said. ''Hey,'' he called, leaping up for the microwave. ''I almost forgot about my spaghetti.''

''That would be a first,'' Meg said.

CHAPTER TEN

CARA dragged through the next day at work, thankfully a Friday, hiding out in her office as much as possible and counting the hours until she could go home and be alone. Meg and Mark had driven to Houston for a twenty-first birthday celebration of a chum, so she would have the weekend to herself. She was terribly confused and needed the time to come to grips with her dilemma—how to avoid staying under the spell of a man who drove her mad, but whom she loved to pieces.

After a dinner of peanut butter spooned from the jar and half a carton of blueberry yogurt, Cara plopped in front of the TV with a bottle of apple juice. This was what she needed—solitude and a marathon of Garbo films. She would just veg out until her head cleared or until the weekend ended—whichever came first.

The second feature had just started when the phone rang. Cara ignored the ringing. She knew who it was—Wyatt. Well, she wasn't ready to speak with him.

To her irritation, the phone continued to interrupt every ten to twenty minutes. Finally, unable to stand it any longer, Cara picked it up. ''Hello?''

"Are you busy?"

"Yes."

"Too busy for me to come over?"

"Yes. Call me tomorrow, Wyatt. Or the day after that. Goodnight." She hung up and returned to her movie.

It wasn't a half hour before the doorbell chimed. Darn. Didn't that man understand simple English? Apparently not, because here he was at the front door in crisp sport shirt and chinos, and smelling of aftershave. "We have unfinished business. May I come in?"

"No."

"OK, have it your way then. We'll do this on the front porch. Cara—" Wyatt cleared his throat. "I want to marry you, take care of you forever." Reaching into the pocket of his pants, he pulled out a black velvet jeweler's box. "This is for you." He placed it in her hand.

Slowly Cara opened the box. Inside was a huge pear-shaped diamond—at least six or seven carets— mounted on a platinum band. "This is ghastly," she snapped, shoving the ring back at him.

"Not exactly the reaction I was hoping for." Wyatt flipped open the lid and stared down at the ring. "I suppose it is a little showy—"

"A little showy? It's downright obscene. And it proves how little you know about me. That ring doesn't say 'I love you.' It says 'Property of Wyatt McCauley, hands off.'"

"Then I missed the mark farther than I thought. I *wanted* it to say 'I love you.'" He slipped the box back into his pocket. "We can choose another one together."

"No, we can't."

"I love you, Cara, and I intend to marry you."

"You're doing it again. I'm beginning to wonder if you've got some kind of brain lock."

"Want to translate for me?"

"No. If you can't figure it out after all I've said, you're hopeless."

Wyatt ran his fingers through freshly combed hair. "Dammit all, Cara, you'll make a mental case out of me yet."

"Then maybe we can get a group rate for therapy, cause you've sure addled my brain. In the meantime, take that ring back to wherever you bought it and let me be."

"OK," he said, "I'm going. Only, understand this. We are getting married. It may take you a while to get used to the idea," Wyatt added, backing away from her, "but once it grows on you, you're going to be as happy about that prospect as I am."

He was halfway down the walk by the time Cara found her tongue again. She darted after him. "Do you think all it takes is for you to announce your intentions and the deed's done? I'm astonished you didn't provide the date and place for this purported wedding. That you haven't already booked the caterer."

"Not yet, I'm still working on that," Wyatt said sarcastically. Words about happy notwithstanding, he sounded like anything but an enthusiastic bridegroom-to-be.

"Save yourself the effort," she barked. "Because even if you schedule the big event for my front yard, *I* won't be there. This proposal is simply another example of your high-handed methods. You expect the whole world to dance to your tune, Wyatt McCauley. Well, sorry, but I'm tired of dancing. I'm sitting this one out."

"Quit acting like I've insulted you," he grumbled. "Plenty of women would be happy to marry me."

"Marry one of *them* then, but I'll wager that most would prefer to be asked rather than told."

"So that's it? You're standing on a technicality? What do you want, a guy who'll drop to his knees and beg for your hand."

"Of course not. But a little romance—a request instead of an order—wouldn't be amiss. Why can't you see that's the crux of our problem? A woman with a modicum of gumption doesn't want her every move dictated by some overbearing oaf who assumes he knows best."

Wyatt raised his eyes to the heavens, as if seeking divine inspiration. "It's clear that nothing I say or do tonight is going to get a reasonable reaction—"

"Reasonable?" Cara threw her arms in the air furiously. "Listen, mister, you're the one without a clue."

"Obviously." Wyatt glowered, then whirled around and stalked to his car.

Cara stood there, her mouth agape, watching him drive off without looking back. Her eyes misted. The last twenty-four hours had been some of the worst of her life.

Wyatt turned the corner, out of view of the Breedon house, and pulled to the curb, sitting there with his fingers beating a tattoo against the steering wheel. He'd committed a major goof—well, two or three, if one was keeping track. The ring, bringing up marriage when Cara was so irate, and then forgetting to actually ask her to be his wife.

How could he have been so stupid? Marriage proposals weren't exactly part of his repertoire, but that didn't excuse his approaching Cara in such a bumbling manner. Her anger was justifiable. If it would do any good, he'd dash back to her house, plead insanity, and beg for forgiveness and another chance.

But Cara wasn't in a forgiving mood at the moment. Not even close. So what was he going to do about it? Give up? He smiled ruefully. Wyatt McCauley was no quitter. He wasn't about to walk away from something he wanted as badly as he wanted Cara. That crazy, stubborn, wonderful, darling woman was going to marry him if it took every ounce of his time and energy to convince her.

The quiet of the weekend ended early Sunday with the arrival of Meg and Mark back from Houston.

"Tell me everything about the party," she said to them.

Excitedly the two relayed the details of the festivities and of people there whom Cara would remember. After a half hour of party talk, Meg turned to Cara. "By the way, has anything happened on the Wyatt front while we were gone? Did you patch up that little disagreement?"

"Oh, Wyatt had a remedy for that. Then again, Wyatt's got a remedy for everything."

Mark propped one hand on the top of the mantel. "From the sound of your voice, this oughta be good. Don't keep us hanging. Tell us the remedy. Although I gather you didn't think much of it."

"He wants to marry me, or so he said. He even had an engagement ring in his pocket. The most aw—"

Meg jumped to her feet. "Why, that's wonderful. I've always known you two were perfect for each other. When's the wedding?" She grabbed Cara's hand. "Where's the ring?"

"I didn't accept it. There's not going to be a wedding. No way will I get hooked up with that…that *man*."

"What about his proposal?" Meg asked, looking distraught.

"What about it? I can't marry Wyatt, honey. I want an equal relationship with a husband and there would never be one with him. The scales don't just tip, they crash in one direction—*his* direction. Wyatt has money, position...why the guy is even prettier than I am."

"So he's wealthy, influential and handsome. You're holding that against him?" Mark asked incredulously.

"Since when have you become such a staunch advocate for Wyatt McCauley?" Cara asked.

"Since I got to know him. Wyatt's a stand-up guy. And he must like us. Why else would he hang around so much?"

"This isn't about *us*, Mark." Cara's pain grew deeper. She'd been so shortsighted letting Wyatt into their lives. Meg and Mark were going to have as hard a time letting go as she was. But Meg and Mark would move on to other pursuits and Wyatt would eventually be forgotten. Cara knew she'd never forget. She'd carry a torch for him until her dying days. "It isn't about *us*," she repeated. "It's about me. As I just told Meg, I can't marry Wyatt. These power trips he's prone to take, the women chasing him—"

"He only wants to be caught by you," Meg reminded.

"Today maybe. What about next week, next month? What chance do we have for a stable marriage?"

"Sounds to me as if you're looking for reasons why it won't work. You ought to give as much time considering why it would."

That uncanny ability of Mark's to sometimes sound like their father sent chills down Cara's spine.

"You love the guy and he loves you," Mark admonished. "It really shouldn't take any more than that."

"You love the guy." Mark's words played in Cara's brain as she tossed and turned that night, anguishing over whether she was wrong and everyone else right. Cara was honest enough to own up to one truth—she hadn't been harmed by Wyatt's abetting and influencing her career. On the contrary, her life had been enhanced. But that still didn't excuse his meddling. Yet as furious as she'd been, Cara was finding it impossible to sustain that fury.

Like it or not, she couldn't bear it if Wyatt were no longer part of her existence. So where did that leave her? Miserable, that's where.

Cara rose the next morning tired and ill-tempered. Determined to put up a good front, she dressed in a bright red suit, one of Meg's newer designs.

The best thing to do was go to work early—before Meg and Mark awoke and began dispensing more unsolicited advice. Once in her office, she'd secrete herself there and try to get her mind off her misery by nonstop work.

She'd just poured a cup of coffee and sat down at her desk when Eliza, her secretary, buzzed her on the intercom. "Cara, you have a delivery. Want me to bring it in?"

"No, I'll come out. Thanks." She pushed her chair back and went to the reception area.

"A hat?" she asked the young man presenting her with a large round box tied with a massive pink bow.

He shrugged. "I just bring them. They don't tell me what's inside. Could you sign on the third line, please?"

Cara balanced the box on her hip and signed the receipt, then set the box on the corner of Eliza's desk, slipped off the bow and eased off the lid to peek inside. In a flash, she slammed the lid closed.

"So was it a hat, ma'am?" The carrier's hand was stuck out for a tip.

She didn't answer, tempted to tell him to return the package to its sender. Instead, she borrowed a dollar from Eliza, slapped it in his palm, then gathered up the box and bow and rushed to her office. Once alone, she opened the box again. The contents hadn't changed. Back on went the lid and the box was shoved on top of her filing cabinet.

But Cara couldn't forget it. After trying for a full minute, she got up, checked to make sure her office door was locked, crossed to the window and shut the blinds. That done, she brought the box to her desk, eased off its top and pulled out the most exquisite wedding veil she'd ever seen—a delicate headpiece of pearls and yards and yards of diaphanous netting. Nestled in the net was a card. "Think you can find a gown to match? I love you. Wyatt."

Cara couldn't resist. She pulled a mirror from her

purse. "What can it hurt?" she said aloud as she slipped the veil on her head. "No, this hairdo will never do. Something upswept." This was crazy, she warned herself. Letting images of white dresses and fairy-tale weddings interfere with her good sense.

Wyatt was just trying to manipulate her once more. A skill he'd mastered all too well.

At ten she was paged again. Another delivery at Eliza's desk. This time Cara grabbed some money for tipping and repaying Eliza. The second gift was a beautifully wrapped package from Neiman-Marcus in Dallas. Cara wondered how Wyatt'd arranged this, considering store hours. But he had. She couldn't suppress a smile. A pattern was developing here.

"Is today your birthday?" Eliza asked as Cara retrieved the package. "I thought it was in January."

"It is. This is simply someone's idea of a practical joke."

Closing her door behind her, Cara opened the package. A designer silk scarf. "Perfect for a honeymoon outfit," said the enclosed card. "Oh, Wyatt," Cara murmured, pressing the card to her lips, "what will you come up with next?"

She soon found out. At noon there was a tap on her door. "You've got a visitor," Eliza announced with an ear-to-ear grin as she ushered in a white-coated waiter pushing a serving cart. A second waiter followed, his hands wrapped around a silver cooler containing a bottle of wine.

Even if Cara was drawing more speculation from

her co-workers than she wanted, she couldn't help but be amused. If Wyatt kept up this treatment, she was a goner.

The two waiters began with a centerpiece of delicate violets and two slender tapers in a matching hue, then laid out a lunch fit for a queen—herbed chicken, creamed dill potatoes, tender green asparagus, chocolate mousse. The card left beside her plate said, "Wouldn't this be even nicer shared with me?"

As she pushed the cart out an hour later, Cara told Eliza, "I suspect they'll return for this soon."

"Are you sure it's not your birthday?"

"Positive. Like I said, just someone's idea of a joke."

"I wish I knew a fellow with a sense of humor like that. What are you expecting next? I am assuming it's a *he* who's responsible."

"It's a he. And considering we've been visited about every two hours so far, I'd say we'll find out what's next before long."

But Cara was wrong. Two hours passed, then two and a half. No more deliveries. She'd begun to think she could see right through Wyatt. He was mimicking their early encounters. The veil—the hat. The scarf—the tie. A gourmet French meal in place of a Tex-Mex lunch.

But now she was confused. Surely Wyatt hadn't forgotten her last gift—the roses? Couldn't he recall their first actual meeting? Cara could recite every detail of it. How she'd had difficulty taking her eyes off him, how she'd fallen in love that very day...

Yes, fallen in love. The instant she'd seen him. The trouble was, she'd spent entirely too much energy telling herself to repress such thoughts, too much energy telling herself Wyatt couldn't possibly love her too. Well if this morning's actions weren't those of a man in love, they were a darn good imitation.

Was the ball in her court? Should she call him? Nah. Wyatt wasn't through yet—he would follow this little project through to the end. Suddenly Cara saw that as endearing. So he was a little controlling. According to Meg and Mark, so was she. Both she and Wyatt could learn some give and take. After all, they were intelligent people. "Where is that man?" she asked out loud.

"She got the veil and the scarf?" Wyatt was sitting on the corner of Frances's desk, fidgeting.

"I verified the deliveries. The lunch arrived on schedule too."

"What did she think?"

"How am I to know? Unlike you, I don't have an in at Sweeney and Winslow."

"She says I'm controlling."

"How long did it take her to figure that out? Two seconds?"

"I've been an idiot, Frances."

"No argument there. But then, love does that to

people. Now get on over there and carry out the rest of your plan.''

"You think it's a good one?''

"I told you this morning it was a good one. Women like romance, women *need* romance. You've served that up to Cara on a giant platter. Frankly, I didn't think you had it in you. I'm proud of you, Wyatt.''

Feeling encouraged, Wyatt straightened his tie, grabbed his jacket and started for Cara's office.

It was almost four when Cara's intercom buzzed again. "You have another visitor,'' Eliza announced.

"Thank heaven.'' Cara rushed out of her office and there he was, half hidden behind the biggest bouquet of yellow roses she'd ever seen. "That's a lot more than the two dozen I gave you.''

"I bought out the florist. Can you spare me a few minutes?''

Oh, yes, she could spare a few minutes. She could spare a lifetime. Cara led Wyatt into her office and closed the door behind them. He laid the flowers on her desk.

"Nice office,'' he began.

"Thank you. Would you like to have a seat?''

"Sure,'' he answered, and they sat in matching chairs, facing one another.

An awkward silence followed before he finally spoke. "Everything you said yesterday was right. I am controlling. I act before I think. I want things my own way and it would be a lie to say I regret tampering with the auction results. If I hadn't, then we wouldn't have gotten together.''

Wyatt took her hand. ''But I should have stopped when I was ahead. Intervening in your job search without your knowledge was wrong, and saying I had your best interests at heart doesn't make it OK. I want to promise it will never occur again, but to be honest, I can't be certain. You see I've never been in love before—''

''In love?'' Cara interrupted.

''In love,'' Wyatt repeated firmly. ''I'll love you forever, Cara Breedon.'' He shook his head in amazement. ''I've always ridiculed the notion of love changing a man, but I've certainly changed since we met. My fear of commitment vanished when compared to the prospect of losing you. So who knows, if I work on it—and I swear to you I will—then maybe some of my bad habits will vanish too.''

''You haven't been the only one making mistakes,'' she said, squeezing his hand. ''I was like a porcupine on alert, ready to quill anyone who interfered in the running of my life. After you left last night, Meg and Mark lit into me, pointing out the error of my ways. After that I did some heavy thinking. I've been so insecure, so paranoid you would take over then dump me...I failed to see the obvious— namely that people take care of those they love. And people who love in return are willing to accept that caretaking.''

"So am I forgiven?" Wyatt stood and pulled her into his arms.

"Completely, totally. Can you forgive me, as well?"

"What do you think?" He kissed her gently. "Have dinner with me tonight and we'll put all this in the past."

Wyatt had just left and Cara was leaning against her office door, her head spinning with thoughts of what tonight would bring when the intercom buzzed once more.

"Another delivery," chimed Eliza.

What now? Cara rushed out to see what was going on. Eliza held a satin pillow, a small jeweler's box in the middle. Beside her was Wyatt, backed up by four more of Cara's co-workers.

"One little thing we didn't clear up," Wyatt said. "Thought I'd call on these witnesses to assure you how serious I am." He took her hand and lifted it to his lips for a kiss. "Will you marry me?"

"Oh, yes," Cara answered happily, oblivious to the fact they had an audience.

"Then let's make it official." Wyatt's dark eyes locked on her tawny ones as if he and she were the only two people on the globe. He lifted the box off the pillow and took out a ring. "Do you like this better?"

It was an oval diamond, about two carats, Cara judged, flanked by smaller diamonds.

"Oh, my!"

"If you don't like it, you can choose another."

"Of course I like it. It's the loveliest ring I've ever seen."

"I'm glad I got it right this time. That first one didn't suit you at all. But I wasn't trying to establish ownership with it, like you said. I got all mixed up with bigger is better and—"

She placed her hand over his lips, hushing him. "It's OK."

Wyatt slipped the ring on her finger and kissed her. A soft, tender kiss, a kiss that made Cara suddenly aware of their spectators when the spontaneous applause broke out.

With another kiss to her forehead, Wyatt gestured over his shoulder. "I have permission to do this."

Cara glanced back and saw Cy Winslow. Then Wyatt scooped her into his arms and began marching toward the hall. "What did you do, check out *An Officer and a Gentleman* at the video store on the way home last night?"

"I've been too busy since last night for movies. This is all my own idea."

"You have wonderful ideas, Mr. McCauley."

"Tell all these nice people they're invited to a wedding."

"You're invited to a wedding," Cara shouted as Wyatt carried her toward the elevator.

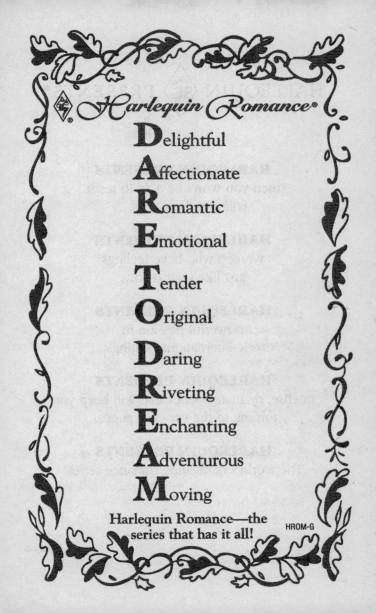

Harlequin Romance®

Delightful

Affectionate

Romantic

Emotional

Tender

Original

Daring

Riveting

Enchanting

Adventurous

Moving

Harlequin Romance—the
series that has it all!

HROM-G

HARLEQUIN PRESENTS®

HARLEQUIN PRESENTS
men you won't be able to resist
falling in love with...

HARLEQUIN PRESENTS
women who have feelings
just like your own...

HARLEQUIN PRESENTS
powerful passion in
exotic international settings...

HARLEQUIN PRESENTS
intense, dramatic stories that will keep you
turning to the very last page...

HARLEQUIN PRESENTS
The world's bestselling romance series!

Harlequin® Historical

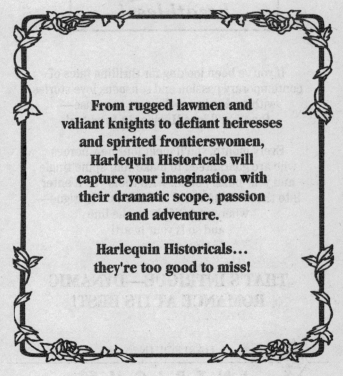

From rugged lawmen and
valiant knights to defiant heiresses
and spirited frontierswomen,
Harlequin Historicals will
capture your imagination with
their dramatic scope, passion
and adventure.

Harlequin Historicals…
they're too good to miss!

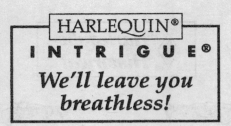

LOOK FOR OUR FOUR FABULOUS MEN!

Each month some of today's bestselling authors bring
four new fabulous men to Harlequin American Romance.
Whether they're rebel ranchers, millionaire power brokers
or sexy single dads, they're all gallant princes—and
they're all ready to sweep you into lighthearted fantasies
and contemporary fairy tales where anything is possible
and where all your dreams come true!

You don't even have to make a wish…
Harlequin American Romance will grant your every desire!

Look for Harlequin American Romance
wherever Harlequin books are sold!

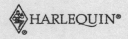

Not The Same Old Story!

 Exciting, glamorous
romance stories that take
readers around the world.

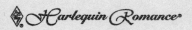 Sparkling, fresh and ten-
der love stories that
bring you pure romance.

 Bold and adventurous—
Temptation is strong women,
bad boys, great sex!

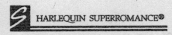 Provocative and realistic
stories that celebrate life
and love.

 Contemporary
fairy tales—where
anything is possible
and where dreams
come true.

 Heart-stopping, suspenseful
adventures that combine the
best of romance and mystery.

 Humorous and romantic stories
that capture the lighter side of
love.